Nicole Locke discovered her first romance novels in her grandmother's closet, where they were secretly hidden. Convinced that books that were hidden must be better than those that weren't, Nicole greedily read them. It was only natural for her to start writing them—but now not so secretly.

Also by Nicole Locke

Lovers and Legends miniseries

The Knight's Broken Promise
Her Enemy Highlander
The Highland Laird's Bride
In Debt to the Enemy Lord
The Knight's Scarred Maiden
Her Christmas Knight

Discover more at millsandboon.co.uk.

RECLAIMED BY THE KNIGHT

Nicole Locke

MILLS & BOON

First published in Great Britain 2018
by Mills & Boon, an imprint of HarperCollins*Publishers*
1 London Bridge Street, London, SE1 9GF

Large Print edition 2018

© 2018 Nicole Locke

ISBN: 978-0-263-07882-4

MIX
Paper from
responsible sources
FSC® C007454

This book is produced from independently certified
FSC™ paper to ensure responsible forest management. For
more information visit www.harpercollins.co.uk/green.

Printed and bound in Great Britain
by CPI Group (UK) Ltd, Croydon, CR0 4YY

This book is dedicated to the wonderful, brilliant, marvellous editors who have helped me along the journey in the Lovers and Legends series. For Linda Fildew, who took a chance on me, for Nicola Caws, who shared her friendship and showed me the ropes, and for Ann-Leslie Tuttle, who welcomed me on my transition to the US.

But especially this book is dedicated to Laurie Johnson, who stuck by me this troublesome year. Nicholas, Matilda and I wouldn't have our happily-ever-after without your unfailing encouragement. I thank you with all my heart and with all my fingers, finally…and happily… dancing across the keyboard once again.

Chapter One

September 1295

The baby kicked low in her belly and Matilda gasped.

'What is wrong?'

She looked at Bess, who was still gleaning the fields and finding any grain that might have been missed in the late harvest. They couldn't spare any food, but even so Matilda was always deeply satisfied when her bag was full. As if she'd been on a treasure hunt and could now feed her family and friends.

'She's kicking me again.'

'It's a girl today?'

Matilda thought about the sharp pain when she'd climbed out of bed that morning, the constant turning of the baby inside her, so that she'd

barely been able to get bread down during breakfast, and now the deep thumping, like a rabbit
in the woods.

'Unquestionably, the baby is a girl.' She pushed
herself off the ground and pressed one hand to
her lower back.

It wasn't the first time she had been punched
on the inside today, and she knew it wouldn't be
the last. The gleaning forced her to remain in
the same position, and the baby demanded that
she stretch. Her giving in to the kick was a com-
promise she happily made, though the reprieve
wouldn't last long.

There was more work to be done, and the
fields were full of families who were stuffing
their sacks. Nearby Agnes, the cordwainer's only
daughter, was crawling on the ground. Unlike
the other children, however, she was taking the
wheat shafts and stacking them like houses.
Matilda wondered which of her brothers would
ruin her creations first.

Bess stood and stamped her feet. 'If your reasoning holds true, the baby will be a girl.'

'You think my certainty is ridiculous?'

'Unlike you, I listen to our healer, Rohesia, who insists you're carrying too low in your belly for a girl. Plus, the only reason you hold this belief is because of your own mischievous past and Roger's temperament—' Bess clamped her mouth shut.

'Do not worry,' Matilda said.

There was only one reason why worry ever crossed Bess's face, and that was if she believed she'd hurt another. Matilda did hurt, but not because her friend had remarked on her husband. She hurt because he was gone.

'Forgive me.' Bess clapped her hands to her cheeks. 'I keep forgetting.'

Matilda saw Bess's dismayed face and felt her own emotions turn inside her again. She was familiar with it. Grief that she hadn't dared release.

'There is nothing to forgive,' Matilda said. 'It's been barely two full moons.'

She'd hurt more if no one mentioned Roger at all. That man, her childhood friend and her husband, deserved to be remembered. He had certainly deserved more than her as a wife. But there was no wishing for that now.

Bess exhaled and shook her head. 'I've made it worse.'

Only for a moment. The least Matilda could do, was give her daughter her father's even temperament. To that end, she was determined her daughter would know no sorrow, and that included her mother's.

Swallowing hard, Matilda said, 'As usual. Now all I have to do is wait until you say something *truly* grievous.'

Bess's lips twisted wryly. 'Give me a few moments.'

Matilda clasped her friend's hand. 'I'm gladdened that you forget he is gone. It will keep him alive when the baby comes.'

Bess's eyes softened as she glanced at Matilda's swollen stomach. 'Anything you wish.'

'Good. Though I try to be calm, I fear she'll need all the gentle temperament she can get. She would do well to remember her father.'

Roger, her best friend and her husband, had been the exact opposite of her. Whereas she, in her youth, had always been taking risks and pulling pranks, Roger had been helpful and protective. Ever easy with his smiles and his care, Roger had been the absolute antithesis of the person she'd been, but she'd wanted his calmness in her life, and he...he'd wanted *her*.

Any moment she'd be crying, and then her friend would believe she had in fact hurt her.

A couple of blinks of her eyes and she saw a familiar figure on the horizon. 'Louve's on his way here.'

Bess turned. 'It's too early for the men to break from the harvesting.'

Glancing towards the sun, Matilda said, 'Apparently not.'

'Then something must be wrong.'

Feeling the same sense of urgency, Matilda placed her hand on her belly and locked her legs. There'd be no running for her.

'There'd be others with him if there was something amiss,' Matilda said.

Even after all this time it went against her instincts to hold still, but when Roger had died, for the sake of her baby, she'd vowed she'd be more like him. To set an example that would serve her child well and never to never turn out like her mother. Foolish. Heartbroken. Alone. Twice now.

Bess lifted her skirts. Despite her girth, she'd be able to run if there truly was an emergency. 'Maybe they couldn't be spared.'

'And Louve can?' Matilda answered. 'At this time of day he must want to discuss the usual problems. Some argument or a missing tally stick.'

'You do too much, and with only two of you now overseeing everything it's not tenable.'

'We'll find a replacement soon enough.'

Until Roger's death there had been three on the estate who oversaw the operations. Now there were only two—herself and Louve, who was both steward for the state and reeve to oversee the crops. She saw to the management of Mei Solis as well as helped settle disputes. Although since Roger—

No. In the fields all day, she thought too much of her lost husband.

Giving in, she strode towards Louve, hoping her mud-caked skirts would slow her enough to give the impression of serenity.

'What is it?' she asked.

Louve indicated behind him. 'I came to warn you. Storm's coming from just beyond that hill.'

She looked over his shoulder towards the field, where the men were cutting the stalks. If there was a storm, the hill disguised it. All around her were clear blue skies. And even if there was a storm, it shouldn't bring Louve here.

Their arrangement was unconventional, but it worked. When lord of Mei Solis manor Nicholas had left to seek the fortune the estate so desperately needed, it had seemed reasonable to leave his friends and Matilda, his betrothed in charge. After all, he had intended to return within two years.

That had been six years ago, and in that time he had broken their betrothal. Despite this, they had kept to the managing arrangement because the manor, families and friends had prospered. She had married Roger, and even if her reputation had been whispered about, her authority on settling disputes and ensuring that Roger and Louve could come to terms had never been questioned.

'Tell me why you're truly here,' she said.

Maybe Bess was right and something was

wrong. On a day like today every man was needed to harvest the last of the crops. Louve was one of the strongest and quickest at the sickle, and every reaper was required.

'I see no storm, and even if there was one, one of the boys could run and tell us that.'

Louve shrugged. 'None of the boys wanted to protect their hands from blisters. I, however, have many reasons to pamper my hands.'

'For the hordes of women after you, no doubt,' Bess interjected.

Matilda almost snorted.

'Exactly. I'd be useless to the women if my hands were wrapped,' he said, with a curve to his lips.

Everything about Louve tended to be irreverent, even in the direst circumstances. It was part of his frustrating charm. That coupled with his exceptional blue eyes and black hair made him the most pursued male she'd ever known. Though lately his attention seemed only for the widow Mary.

'I know exactly what the women would think about your uselessness,' Bess quipped. 'They'd be overjoyed not to be harassed by the likes of you.'

'Ah, Bess, still pining for me, as always.'

Bess and Louve had been teasing each other like this for years. Bess, older than them both, was already married with a grown child.

'That's me—still waiting for you to get some sense. It appears I'll have to keep waiting.'

'Well, you know where to find me.'

Bess nodded. 'Lazily talking with us when you should be reaping the wheat like the other men.'

Somewhere along the way Louve had picked up Matilda's bag and swept more grain into it. It was then that his intent became irritatingly clear. 'Are you here for *me*?'

Louve's mouth quirked. 'I'm here to save the grain. Storm's coming.'

Louve was doing *her* work. The skies were still blue; there was no storm coming. 'You can't do this.'

Louve smiled ruefully. 'You're working too hard now.'

'And the baby *is* kicking,' Bess added.

'Are you on *his* side now?' Matilda said. 'I'm

working because there's work to be done. Crops are better this year, so there's more gleaning.' A fact that had them all breathing a sigh of relief.

'That sack's getting too heavy for you to carry.'

She looked at the ground, thought of running horses to try and calm herself. When that didn't work, she narrowed her eyes on Louve. 'I'll say this differently. I *won't* have you do my work for me.'

'Roger would have—'

Matilda held up her hand and shook her head firmly.

'Oh, dear,' Bess whispered.

But Matilda ignored her friend for now. She would also ignore all references to her husband. He was too recently gone, and though she wanted her baby to know of him, her baby couldn't hear yet. Right now she didn't want to be reminded of Roger's protective nature when he could no longer protect.

'It may be true…what he would have wanted… but I'm here now, and my crawling on this ground is a duty I need to fulfil. I'm not helping with the binding. I'm here with the children, gleaning.'

'Stubborn as usual. What kind of reputation will I have if I can't move a pregnant woman? I'll never hear the end of it,' Louve said.

'You ruined your reputation when you were four years old, Louve, and you know it,' Bess said. 'And it appears—

Shouts came from behind them. A young boy was racing over the hill. His cries were carrying on the autumnal breeze.

'Did he say we have company?' Bess said.

Matilda turned her ear to the boy's words, but they were still too faint. No one visited the estate. Up until this year they had been the ones who travelled to other villages and other markets to sell their wares. However, if the crops stayed this plentiful that would change. Until then...

Panting, the boy stopped in front of them.

'We have guests arriving?' Matilda cradled her belly, supporting the baby, who was blessedly still now that she'd given her room.

'Visitor,' the boy clarified. 'With two giant horses behind him!'

The world...the ground underneath Matilda... shifted.

'Steady,' Bess whispered, grabbing her elbow.

'How far out?' Louve asked the boy.

'Just outside the barren fields.'

If they could see a rider coming in that direction it meant he came from the east.

Louve glanced from Bess to Matilda and then back. 'I'm closer than the others. I'll get a horse and greet him before he reaches the trees.'

There was nothing to be discussed. It was the only choice, given all the men were in the opposite direction and she couldn't move her legs.

Matilda kept her eyes on Louve's long stride, taking him to the stables. 'I will be well,' she whispered. 'Just give me moment more.'

Bess kept her hand where it was. 'You knew this day would come.'

Matilda placed her hand on top of Bess's. It was true. She had always known this day would come. Like a storm and the changing seasons. Like the endless rising of the sun and the setting of the moon. Like the certainty of time. She had known she'd see Nicholas again.

'Always.'

Chapter Two

Nicholas rode guardedly towards his home, his father's prison and the cause of his death. Mei Solis Manor. Ridiculous name: *My Sun.*

It had been a grand gesture from an impoverished knight to his new wife, Helena of Catalonia, the sixth daughter from a family who'd gained wealth in maritime, but no title. His father, a mere knight with a crumbling manor, had had favour and connections with the English Court, and thus had been able to wed a woman of some means.

Such happy news upon his father's return. His father had been beaming with pride, knowing that with silver the rich soil estate would prosper with the right management and supplies.

Nicholas, six years old at the time, remembered the day Helena had arrived. His father had toiled for months before, and the estate had never looked better. When the carriage had stopped, his father, eschewing custom, had assisted his new wife in alighting from the carriage.

Chin raised, a tight smile on her face, she had stood next to his father. Her gown, almost white, had seemed to glow, made of some fabric he had never seen before. His first and only thought at the sight at his new mother had been, *The sun's light never stays*.

He had been right. Helena had had only a modest income from her doting family, and had shared most of her dowry with her new husband and his estate. The remainder had been used for her return to London and Court, where she had remained despite his father's attempts to make the manor more hospitable for her and his pleading messages. She had stayed there despite his own curt message regarding her husband's sudden death.

After his father had died Nicholas had seen Helena a few times at Court. She had always been surrounded, but they had exchanged polite greetings given the agreement between them. After all, his father had paid with his life to keep the estate running, and Nicholas had paid Helena with his coin ever after to keep her well-dressed.

It was an arrangement made by his father that he continued. It was his sentence and his prison, too. As long as he paid Helena there would never be enough coin.

There'd been clear blue skies since he'd left London to travel west to his home, but the easy weather and the ride hadn't alleviated the tumultuousness of his memories or the brutal facts. It had taken him six years to get enough coin. Six years during which he'd lost everything. His friends, his eye, his only love.

In the distance, a different shape arose from the empty peaks and valleys. At first it was too small to comprehend, but as it grew he recognised the lone rider. A friend to greet him.

Not that any greeting would be welcome. He'd never intended to return here. He wouldn't be here at all except that he'd made a promise to a fellow mercenary to repair his past.

However, the only repair he could conceive

of was to exact revenge on the three who had betrayed him. Something, no matter how much pain had been caused to him, he had never been able to bring himself to do.

Yet here he was, travelling alone on a road he'd never wanted to take, intending to do just that. All because his friend had reclaimed his past, found happiness, and requested that Nicholas do the same.

He'd stay the winter at his former home with its ridiculous name, find some justice from the people who'd blindsided him, and then be gone again. With any hope he'd be free of the painful memories of betrayal and be able to find his future.

So revenge he must have. The acts done to him were far past reparation and apology. His hatred of those deeds was the only emotion that had fuelled him for the last three years. There was nothing to reclaim or repair for him. Anything of worth in his past had been lost. He could gain nothing from nothing. Mei Solis was a vast emptiness to him. *My Soulless.*

Even recognising his childhood friend, Louve,

as he neared wasn't enough to gladden him. Not when he saw him pull up short, causing the horse to skitter backwards. Louve was a master horseman. The only reason for this lack of control was because he'd got a good look at Nicholas's face and it had shocked him.

His scar. For years now he'd had it. A sword-swipe that had begun across his belly and moved up to his chest, and then the flick of an enemy's wrist that had projected the sword-tip across his face and destroyed his left eye.

All sewn and beautifully stitched now, it was only a slight silvery shadow of the horror it had once been. The horror it still was, since his left eyelid would never rise again. But it was also a blessing, because it permanently covered the fact that he could no longer see on that side.

It was a battle wound that had made his sword-training fiercer and his battle mien more menacing. In the mercenary business, such a scar benefited him. But here, as the lord of a genteel manor, it was a liability. Now he would have to suffer questions, skirt the truth, or tell lies about how he'd received it. There would be gasps of dismay and horror, and—worse—pity.

He knew this, and though he'd worn no patch since his accident, he wore one now, for the trip home. The patch covered the worst of it, and yet still Louve's horse skittered at the sudden jerk of his master's reins.

He'd only just set foot on his land and had a fair distance to go before he reached the manor. He'd hoped for a brief reprieve until then, so he could see how his land fared. Instead, one of his oldest friends—one of those who'd betrayed him—had ridden out to greet him and almost toppled his horse as a result.

He didn't want this.

Nicholas held his horse steady as Louve settled his. Neither man lowered his gaze. When Louve dismounted, so did he. For just that time Nicholas let Louve gawk at his injury.

He studied Louve as well, and noticed minor changes. His dark hair was longer, and he had more strength to him. But the irreverent look in his eyes, the way he held himself as if the world was a joke—that was painfully familiar.

Another moment passed and then Louve's lips pursed and he whistled low. 'You dumb bastard. You've returned but you've forgotten your eye.'

Nicholas was a liar. He was damned *glad* to see Louve—but that didn't mean he liked it. Whatever friendship they had once shared had been battered away.

But what to do about it? Strike him down? Shove a sword through his guts? *Nothing.* He would do nothing right now. The disquiet coursing through him over coming here was gone, only to be replaced by a burning frustration at the injustice of liars and thieves.

'Well, I can't go back for it,' Nicholas said, gauging this man's reactions. Louve wasn't Roger, or Matilda, but still he'd played his part. Something would have to be done.

'I suppose we'll have to take you as you are?' Louve asked.

And there was the crux. *He* was the lord of this manor, and he'd been sending coin to make Mei Solis prosperous again. But he'd given the control of his home to two men and a woman. Despite the law, this man *did* have a say as to whether he could return. Which was one of the reasons why Nicholas had not written to inform anyone of his intended homecoming.

When Nicholas shrugged, Louve took the steps necessary to pound his aching back and shake him—briefly and far too roughly.

Unexpected. Unwanted. Nicholas stepped away from his touch.

Louve's easy manner fell, and he gathered his horse's reins.

Refusing to ease Louve's feelings, Nicholas grabbed his horse's reins and stepped in beside him.

'Could you look any worse?'

A joke. Did Louve think to make light talk, as if six years didn't separate them? What was his game?

'I asked the bastard to take the other eye, but he couldn't because I'd killed him.'

Louve raised one brow. 'So you decided to wear some pauper's unwashed clothes to finish the look instead?'

Wearing a rich man's clothes would get him killed. 'I've travelled far.'

'Alone?' Louve eyed the other tethered horses, which carried large satchels.

Nicholas knew Louve would guess there was coin in there, and he was right.

'Just since London. Are we walking to the manor?' It was miles yet, and he'd ridden hard since London.

'If we ride we'll be there in a few minutes. Walking gives us time to talk.'

A conversation amongst friends?

A part of him wanted to toss Louve to the ground and demand to know why he hadn't stopped Matilda's marriage. Why he hadn't at least written to him, warn him. No, it was too soon. He would make them reveal their game first, before he revealed his.

'I've written you letters almost every month for the last six years.'

'True, but I notice the lack of any letter informing us of your return. We'll probably never hear the end of it from Cook. But I have to admit the coin you sent was convenient.'

'*Was* it?'

He was too far away to see the village or his

home. Mei Solis was an open field manor. In the centre of his land was the manor itself, with a small courtyard and some buildings for his own private use, such as his stables. A simple gate kept his property separate from the village and from the tenants that encircled the manor for their own protection. Surrounding everything were fields for livestock and crops. All he could see so far was this road, which was narrow and rough, and useless fallow fields.

It stung to return here and be so brutally reminded of his failed past. He might have lost his eye, but while he'd been gone he'd gained balance, and a sense of worth as a mercenary. He'd gained friends—and wealth as well. And yet he was not even a furrow's length on his land and the weight of his past burdens cloaked him again.

'Your coin was quite handy. I'd be pleased to show you how,' Louve said. 'You are staying, I presume?'

Was Louve's game to pretend to be friends? Maybe he thought to put Nicholas at ease so he would return to his mercenary life and leave them alone.

A dark, insidious thought came. Matilda had married Roger, but maybe she'd had Louve as well. What did *he* know? He'd thought she was true to him, as he had been to her. But her marrying Roger had proved she was as faithless as his stepmother had been. And Roger's and Louve's lack of correspondence depicted men without honour. *All* were without honour.

As such, if he did nothing else he would put no one at ease and tell nothing of his intentions. 'Since I can barely feel my legs, I will stay until they can carry me again.'

Louve shot his gaze over to him, but Nicholas pretended not to see it.

'I suppose that's more information than we've had in the past,' Louve said, after several more moments.

'Not good enough?' Nicholas said.

'You're as surly as a wolf in winter, but I understand why.'

So he should, thought Nicholas.

'She's out in the fields now,' Louve remarked.

She. Matilda. It was late harvest time, and he could envisage her there. Her red-gold hair shining brighter than any crop. Her hazel eyes lit with more colours than a field of green. Matilda— who at one point in his life had meant everything to him, who had been his very soul.

Then she had broken her promise to him and betrayed him in the cruellest of manners. He'd returned to Mei Solis to fix his past. He intended to meet it head-on and bury it.

But he kept his head turned away from Louve, though he could feel his former friend's gaze. 'Let's take the horses to the manor,' Nicholas said.

Matilda should have heard their voices or the extra commotion in the yard. She should have heard *his* voice. But she couldn't seem to hear anything through the roaring in her head. Not even her own thoughts were clear to her.

She realised that Bess, who walked beside her, hadn't been as affected as her. Bess had understood that Nicholas was within a few paces on their path and hadn't steered them in another direction.

But it was too late for her, because Nicholas was suddenly there before her. Already handing his reins to a boy, with whom he shared a few words.

He faced away from her, and his back afforded her a few moments to watch him while he exchanged greetings and soothed one of his horses, who stamped his hooves as the satchels were removed.

Nicholas. How had she forgotten how formidable he was? His brown hair was much longer, and tied back in a *queue* which emphasised his shoulders, so much broader than when he'd left six years ago. From being a mercenary; from swinging his sword and killing.

Such a dangerous and unscrupulous profession had given him the strength she saw in his arms, in the tapering of his waist to the defined legs that had walked the many lands he'd once written to her about.

The horses he'd chosen were huge, but they

didn't disguise what a giant of a man he was. How had she forgotten the *immensity* of him?

Bess went still at her side, neither pushing her forward nor turning her away, while others offered shouts and greetings. Not all the voices held joy. There was a tenor of dismay that she couldn't understand.

Surely sounds of distress had no meaning when the prodigal lord of the manor had returned. Now was a time for joy and much celebration. If Nicholas had returned, it meant he'd fulfilled his vow to his people. It meant he had enough funds to make Mei Solis all he'd envisaged and promised.

Or perhaps he had simply returned without coin. How was she to know? He had once been so honourable in his vows...and then he had broken the vow he'd made to her. To make her his wife.

He turned then, deliberately, as if her accusations had struck his back. When he fully faced her, even Bess's hand at her elbow didn't steady her.

She swallowed a gasp as she noticed his left

eye was covered by a brown leather patch. But otherwise, how could she have forgotten how he looked? The angles of his jaw softened only by the fullness of his lower lip. The broadness of the nose he'd boasted no one could ever break? How his steady brown gaze had riveted her?

She remembered their kisses. The way he'd smelled and felt when he'd held her. And his gaze…the way he'd looked at her. But she'd forgotten the feeling of breathlessness from just his look. It was this that had captured her when they'd been only friends. It was his gaze that had made him see into her soul and she into his as they fell in love.

What did he see in her right now? Almost eight months pregnant, her skirts saturated with mud, wheat stuck in her hair. Shock in her eyes, trembling in her limbs, and her breath coming short.

Shorter yet as she comprehended why her heart pounded so desperately until her breath wouldn't come. Why her nerves jarred her inside as if trying to wake her.

Nicholas had a scar across his face. A thin slice that went from his left temple across his left eye, and down his cheek. Then there was a gap at his neck, before a broader gash revealed itself on his collarbone and disappeared under his loose tunic. He'd tried to cover his eye with brown leather, but she could see it. As if in a nightmare, she could see all of it.

All these years she'd imagined the swing of a sword gutting him. Imagined him spilling his life's blood in a field too far away for her to reach him. He was here—alive—but he had lost his eye. What he must have suffered…

And she hadn't known. He'd never told her. Hot rage roared through her, until her first and only instinct was to hit and rail at him and never stop. How could he have done this to himself? How could he have done this to *her*?

His brows drew in and his mouth grew fierce. His gaze, as open as hers must have been, grew cold. What did he see in her eyes?

Too much. She had purposely forgotten how he could see too much. How he *knew* her. And she'd thought she'd known him. Until the day he'd left Mei Solis. Until the moment he'd stopped writing to her and forgotten her completely.

She'd held on until her mother's death, when she had realised how fleeting life was and that she should not wait a moment longer. So she'd agreed to marry Roger, and now she carried their baby. A daughter who was now more important than ever.

She briefly closed her eyes to Nicholas. Heard the horses being led away and Louve's chatter regarding the weather. She focused on Bess's clenching grip on her elbow, on the calls of children and animals, the smell of freshly cut wheat.

She was here on Mei Solis, the home that had remained her home because *she* had stayed, and she drew strength from it.

Nicholas was standing, waiting. It seemed the whole courtyard was waiting.

For her to throw something at him? To yell? To burst into hysterics or give a cutting remark because she was a woman scorned?

In their youth she had been mischievous and he reckless. They'd appeared a perfect match in every way. They'd shown no caution in their courtship because they'd seen no need to. And then he'd left because of his restlessness and his ideas of grandeur, even as she had begged for him to stay.

Six years. And now not only her but the entire courtyard held its breath for this reunion.

But she wouldn't rail or hit out—though that had been her first response. Between that breath and now she had found strength from her home. She had purposely changed herself over these last few years and was no longer the woman he had left. No longer the girl he'd grown up with, when they had been friends.

Friends. They had been friends first—before they'd held hands, kissed and promised to marry each other. Before she'd given him her heart and almost her body. Before he'd left and broken her trust.

Friends since childhood. And he had meant the world to her as they'd run and raced and jumped and laughed.

If that boy stood before her now, what would she do?

Striding over, she lifted herself on her toes and gave him a brief embrace before stepping back beside Bess. 'Welcome home, Nicholas,' she said, pleased that her voice did not break on his name. That her gaze stayed steady with his. 'Are you hungry?'

He stood as still as the manor behind him, while she placed her hands on her belly as if to comfort her baby. Only she knew the truth of who truly needed comfort.

His gaze took in her movement and held there for only a moment. Her gown was heavy, and hid most of her pregnancy, but the protective cupping of her hands and their weight against her gown showed to anyone how far along she was.

'It's wonderful to be here again,' he said, just as evenly. 'And I am famished. But even I know this isn't the time for food, and I don't wish to inconvenience anyone.'

She only just held back the shudder that went through her. Maybe it wasn't his gaze that had made her fall for him, but the deep roundness of his voice. The rich tone was fitting for a man of his stature, but somehow it had always made him seem more of a giant among men.

But the sound of his voice was something he had no control over. What he said, however, he did. Cold. Formal. As if they were strangers and he was merely visiting.

A slice of anger scored through her at the injustice of his carefully crafted words. Did he think he was putting her in her place? That she was merely someone from his past...perhaps only a servant?

She was more than angered now, but she kept it in check. She wasn't the same Matilda he had so carelessly thrown away.

Rising above her emotions, she said, 'You've returned to your home. It's more than time for food—it's time for a feast.'

Chapter Three

He couldn't breathe. Couldn't hear or see. Whatever words he'd uttered had come from somewhere else, because he couldn't recall what he'd said.

Matilda was more beautiful than he'd ever seen her. The autumn light played warmly against the havoc of gold in her hair. The sun's glow gleamed a beam across her eyes so that they showed more green than brown, and made shadows of her lashes across her reddened cheeks.

Stunned at seeing her, though it was ridiculous to be so surprised, his only response was to stare like a fool and helplessly track the fluttering movement of the hands that had landed on the swell of her belly she so lovingly caressed.

Matilda carried a child not their own.

Whatever agony he'd experienced before was nothing to this. *Nothing.*

And it was made more cruel as Matilda embraced him as if they were long-lost friends. He could feel the weight of her against his chest, smell the scent she carried of fresh-cut wheat. No matter the year, she'd always smelled that way to him—like the promise of abundance.

Pain. Too much. And he wanted to draw his sword against it.

Enough. How much more could she take away from him? He had thought she'd taken it all and left him only the coldness that he'd honed until he was the most lethal of mercenaries.

And yet a mere heartbeat, a glance at her swollen curves, mocked this belief. He wanted to howl against the pain—but an audience surrounded them and she stared expectantly at him.

Did she expect an offer of friendship? Surely everyone here wouldn't expect it? After all, he'd left here as her betrothed, and had toiled for years to make a home worthy of her. When she had decided she'd had enough waiting, she'd married his closest friend and written him a letter.

But he'd kept to his bargain and continued to send coin, so she could keep herself in the manner to which she had become accustomed…just like his stepmother.

He should count himself lucky that he hadn't married Matilda after all. The coldness of her heart would never curse him as Helena's had his father. And Matilda's heart *was* cold—of that he now had evidence.

Nicholas's wound wasn't new to him, but it was to *her*. What he'd suffered…how he'd survived. So much *pain*… And yet she stood calmly before him, asking about his stomach instead of his eye.

If she wished for cold formality, he would treat her in kind. 'I need no feast, nor any warm welcomes,' he said. 'I would not wish to cause you any more burden than that you already carry. I merely need a place to unpack my satchels and to change these clothes. My rooms are still available, are they not?'

There was a crack in her friendly demeanour,

a tightening of her clasped hands. 'They have been meticulously maintained.'

He relished seeing her mask slip. Until he knew how to exact his revenge it was best that she knew her place in his life—she was his bailiff, who managed his manor. 'Then you have done your duties well. Good day.'

He turned, intending to stride away, only to be stopped by others. Greeted. Slowed in making his escape.

Louve was cracking smiles and talking to the tenants who waited to speak with him. In the past he had done much the same. Joked, answered questions, fielded enquiries from the tenants when they had pressured Nicholas too much. When the coin hadn't enough for their demands Louve had learned to distract them so Nicholas could get away.

He wanted to get away now. He could feel Matilda's gaze at his back. He broadened his steps and stormed closer to the manor, his fists clenching, ready for a fight. It took every effort to keep his shoulders and his breath even.

To appear as if nothing was the matter when in actuality a sword had been sunk into his heart.

Did it look to her as if he was retreating? Let her think what she wanted. He didn't care.

Matilda kept her chin high and her eyes on everyone who had observed Nicholas turning his back on her. Shaming her in front of the tenants...*again.*

'Steady...' Bess whispered by her side.

Humiliated, Matilda didn't want Bess's comfort. Keeping her hand on her belly, she walked in the opposite direction from Nicholas. The thick crowds parted easily. Because of her pregnancy or her disgrace?

Damn him for making her think these thoughts. She'd done her duty to the Lord of Mei Solis in greeting—and, more, she'd done her duty to Roger's memory by keeping her composure as he would have done.

But she hadn't wanted to. Not when she had first seen Nicholas, and certainly not after he'd spoken.

She had been cordial. He had not. What right

did he have to treat her like a servant? As if all that mattered to him was that she did her duties here.

He had broken their betrothal and her heart when he had left Mei Solis, when he'd stopped his letters. He had no right to be aggrieved. But she was satisfied that the new Matilda had kept her calm. She'd changed herself, and today was testament that it was for the better. She just needed to distract herself a bit longer...

'We'll need to notify Cook of a feast—'

Bess's hand on her elbow stopped her. 'Be easy. Everyone knows of his return. Cook will already be preparing something special to add to the evening meal. You need to—'

She wouldn't be 'easy' if Bess held her here. 'Then I'll see my father.' She turned sharply to her right and Bess let her go. 'He'll need to know.'

Bess opened her mouth, closed it.

Matilda ignored Bess's enquiring eye. She needed something to do between now and dinner. Something to occupy her hands, if not her thoughts.

She had always known this day would come, but she hadn't been prepared for Nicholas's injury. His patch hid most of the damage to his eye, but a scrap of leather couldn't hide the fact that he'd suffered. The fact he'd never see the world as he had when they were children, when they'd first held hands…

There came the sting of tears, and she stumbled in her walk. She refused to think of Nicholas now. If she gave in to her weakness for him she'd never make it through this first night. He deserved no pity. Six years gone, and his friend dead, and he hadn't even enquired about him.

'My father will need to be prepared, and it's best done by me. You know how he'll feel about this.'

Her father had believed Nicholas would return to Mei Solis and to his daughter. Then her mother had died, and her father…her father hadn't been the same.

'He may not remember. It may be a bad day,' Bess said.

Her mother and father had been very old when she was born, and she didn't know now if it was his age or if losing her mother had caused the gaps in his memory. But he was a proud man, and he needed care, though all the while they made it appear as if they *weren't* caring for him.

'Regardless, it's best I check.'

'You're doing too much,' Bess said, her voice low. 'You should sit. Maybe rest before dinner.'

That was the last thing she needed to do. 'I'll be fine.'

Just a few more steps and they'd be beyond the courtyard's shadow and most of the prying eyes.

Bess sighed. 'There's no screeching coming from his home…that is a good sign.'

'Or Rohesia has bashed his head in with a cauldron.'

'True…'

There were days when Matilda and her father were more enemies than friends, but even if this was one of her father's bad days, she'd gain distraction.

Curse Nicholas for returning. Why now? He'd never acknowledged the letter Roger had sent before they'd married, nor hers which she'd written with such meticulous care after they'd said their vows. The days she'd spent on each word...

Matilda shook herself. She'd put the past behind her and changed her ways. She'd put the Nicholas who was here now at Mei Solis behind her as well.

Too soon, Louve and Nicholas reached the threshold of a room he'd only ever intended to enter again as Matilda's husband, and Louve gazed at him expectantly.

He had no expectations. The tomblike manor, Matilda's cold formality...the fact that Roger hadn't greeted him. He wasn't welcome here.

Matilda was pregnant.

Again he was blindsided. Again betrayed. The blade swiftly planted between his ribs before he had even seen the glint of steel.

How he'd longed for a family with her. How he'd toiled to provide for his future children so they wouldn't have to bear the burdens he had. And now Matilda was pregnant with another man's child.

Boys carrying his personal supplies scampered

past him in a race to reach his rooms before he did. But he didn't need them to remember his way to the rooms that had once been his father's.

All it took was the achingly familiar shape of the corridors that neither time nor distance could erase from his memory. As a boy, he too had scampered down this corridor. As a man, he had closed the door when he'd left for the last time.

He needed to get out of here. Never to have agreed to this fool's errand. Never to have believed for a moment that he could have what Rhain had found with Helissent if he simply repaired his past.

There was no fixing this. He'd faced battles and men with rage in their eyes. He'd thought he could face this. Face her and hear her explanation. Hear Roger's. Even Louve owed him something for not warning him.

Could he stay here just for revenge? He doubted he could stay here for apologies—not after seeing Matilda cradle her belly. Time had passed, and he shouldn't feel the betrayal all over again like in some minstrel's song. But she had stood before him and she hadn't cared that he'd lost his eye. Hadn't flinched at his return.

'I need to change my clothing,' he said, instead of voicing the thoughts roiling through him.

'I'll have water brought up.'

Nicholas pointed to some boys who were carrying pails into the room. 'There are some buckets here.'

'You'll need a tub.'

What he needed was some time to come to terms with Matilda's pregnancy.

'How many more are there?' he asked.

Louve gave him a questioning glance.

Nicholas looked over Louve's shoulder to the flat stone embedded in the wall. The stone he'd mutilated with his first dagger while waiting for his father to emerge from his empty marriage bed.

'She's expecting a child. How many children do they have?'

'*That's* the question you want to ask me? I thought you'd want to talk about—'

'Just answer me, dammit,' Nicholas interrupted.

Louve's gaze turned assessing. 'After six years I thought you'd be prepared.'

It had been only three years since her—*their*—betrayal. 'No, you didn't think that. That's why you're here now—to see what scene I'll make.'

'Why are you here?'

'This is my home. I have every right to be here.' He didn't have to give explanations to anyone.

'You may have a right to be here, but you have no right to ask questions of Matilda's personal well-being.'

'You lecture *me* on what I have a right to?' He knew Louve was as guilty as the others. 'You, Roger and Matilda owe me!'

'Roger? You bring *Roger* into this? You can't even let—'

Without a word or a message, without facing him like a man, Roger had married the only woman he'd ever loved.

'God himself would expect his punishment.'

Louve's jaw dropped. 'You can't—'

'I do.'

But Roger's reckoning would wait until the

coward met him face to face. Nicholas had no intention of sharing words with Louve on Roger's black deeds.

'For now, I'm simply expecting an answer to my question. How many?'

Louve's expression turned mutinous. 'The Nicholas I knew would have shown some mercy towards Roger...towards Matilda, given the circumstances.'

Mercy? To Roger? *Never.* 'Tell me more.'

Louve's brow deepened, then he looked away. 'No.'

'You walked with me up here and now you don't want to talk?'

'You're not—' Louve shook his head. 'You're not asking the right questions, and I refuse to believe you can be such a bastard. Come, let's order some flagons brought up and we can share them here.'

Nicholas flexed his hands at his sides. A bath, ale, banter amongst friends... Were Matilda and Roger supposed to join them as well? *Ridiculous.* He had the answer to his question and these people were no longer his friends.

'I have no patience to gossip like an old woman.'
He closed the door in Louve's face.

'What could possibly detain him?' Matilda asked, not for the first time.

The meal was prepared, and most of the tenants had arrived. Many were dressed in their best clothes in honour of Nicholas's return. Many had come tonight, and the Great Doors continued to let in icy wind and any stray animal that was fast enough to bypass the children trying to block them.

'I left him upstairs…' Louve shrugged.

That had been hours ago, and all day she'd found no distraction. The tenants, her friends, all were excited by Nicholas's return. Yet she couldn't—wouldn't—join in their happy exclamations or murmured conversations.

Her father had been sleeping while Rohesia crushed herbs. Her home had been empty, just as she'd left it. So she had swept her clean floor as if she was attacking wasps and not her turbulent thoughts until she was exhausted. She was always tired now, and even more so when she thought of Roger and what he'd think about today.

What would he make of the joyful chatter spinning through the winding lanes? Mere months he'd been gone. Not enough for grief to be less, but somehow enough for her to feel lost.

She missed her friend…the man who'd wanted her when no one else did. No amount of sweeping would erase that. But then she'd slept long and arrived here late—only to discover the lord of the manor hadn't shown.

'He closed the door in your face and you let him?'

'What would you have had me do?'

What had they done in the past? She couldn't remember. The boys had seemed to have their own mysterious ways. Their chores, their training, their missions and lessons.

'Perhaps you could have stayed with him.'

'The man sought rest. I had no intention of watching him bathe or sleep.'

Six years was enough to make a man grown. It had happened to Roger and to Louve. Of course it had happened to Nicholas as well.

Unbidden came thoughts of Nicholas asleep in that room, his dark brown hair curled along his shoulders and spread against the dark cover she'd chosen. His body half turned, as if waiting for her to wake him.

She closed her eyes to hide the sudden sharp emotion before Louve guessed her thoughts. 'He's been gone so long and is probably in want of glad tidings. That is all I meant.'

'Why, Matilda, it sounds like you *care*.'

She narrowed her gaze. 'As bailiff, it is my duty to ensure his comfort. And I am one of his oldest friends.'

Louve rolled the cup in his hand. 'Are you still friends with him?'

'Why would I not be?' She had done nothing wrong. Roger would want her to let the past be the past. Roger had been her future...or as much as she had let him be.

'I offered to share ale, if that appeases your sense of hospitality.' Louve gestured with the cup in his hand.

That was good, except... 'But he closed the door in your face.'

'He didn't stay in that room.'

'I don't understand…'

'I hadn't made it far down the stairs before I heard his additional requests. He had them move the buckets to the adjoining room. I didn't stay to find out the reason. I know when I'm not wanted.'

So did she—and *she* knew what had happened even if Louve had not guessed. Nicholas had rejected that room just as he'd rejected her. She'd spent coin, time…part of her heart…preparing the room for when he returned, for when he claimed his bride.

He'd taken one look at it and desired the adjoining room. Fuming, Matilda tapped her foot. Worse, it showed that the great lord of the manor expected wasteful comforts. He'd make more work for the household…for her as bailiff.

He had been rude to her, rude to Louve. Maybe she went too far in offering him *any* hospitality, despite the fact this was his home and Roger would have wanted her to.

'What did he say about Roger?'

'Nothing.'

She quickly brushed the chill away from her arms. It did little to warm her, and she knew the coldness came from inside her. Because she was failing to hold back her grief. To show charity and patience as Roger would have wanted. As her daughter deserved.

Perhaps Nicholas was too tired…perhaps he wanted the smaller rooms for household ease.

'Were his condolences sincere?' she asked, trying to imagine the conversation.

Louve levelled his eyes at her. 'He said *nothing* of Roger.'

'Roger would—'

Louve's words registered. Matilda unwound her arms and clenched her hands. There was no imagining this. To be that cruel. That cold. Maybe to her, but never to Roger. When Nicholas had left she'd seethed, but Roger had mourned the loss of their friendship. To know that Nicholas didn't feel anything. Had not offered some words of kindness…

'He said nothing of your marriage either,' Louve added.

Something hot seared through her. 'He has

no *right* to talk of my marriage. No right to talk about me or—'

'He did mention—' Louve stopped.

'What did he mention?'

'It doesn't matter.'

Servants swept by with great platters and they sidestepped to give them room. 'You should know better than to ignore me,' Matilda said, lowering her voice.

'You're slower than you used to be.' Louve looked pointedly at the swell in her belly. 'I may be able to get away with it.' At her warning look, he caved. 'He asked about your babe.'

Her baby. Nicholas had already acknowledged her pregnancy when he'd described her child as a burden. 'He has no right to talk of her. I hope you set him right.'

Louve's puzzled expression changed to one of reflection as he eyed her.

She looked away, which was probably telling enough that she didn't need to add bitter words. But she refused to feel this sense of wrongness. 'He should never have returned here.'

'It is his home, Matilda.'

'It's never been his home. All his life he talked of exploring other lands, and eventually he did. There is no reason for him to return.' *She* had been his only reason to return, and eventually she hadn't been enough.

'You may love this crumbling manor and the crooked lanes surrounding it, but it's *his* inheritance.'

'One he never wanted. He earned more coin as a mercenary. You'll see—one winter here will remind him, and off he'll go again.'

'Ready to be rid of me so soon?' Nicholas said, from directly behind her.

Louve was quick to turn, but she held her posture that bit longer, to show her displeasure. Sneaking up behind them meant Nicholas had come from the servants' entrance. They'd thought him asleep and sequestered upstairs. He was already proving difficult—and that had been before he overheard their conversation.

Carefully, she turned, taking in the fine weave of his green tunic, stretched wide against the mounds of his chest, the thick weight of his breeches just skimming the strength in his legs.

The clothes weren't new, but they were a wealthy man's clothing. Tailored for him with a weave so fine that the green almost reflected in the hall's candlelight.

Mei Solis's seamstress had never been able to get the cut of his clothes large enough for him to move properly. But these clothes fitted him so well, it didn't take much to see the man beneath. A glance was all it took to see Nicholas in ways she never had before. Always tall, but never this broad. Never this...*lethal.*

She raised her eyes and took in more of the man. His thick hair was damp and waving loose around his shoulders. His face was now shaven, revealing the cut of his jaw, the sensual slash of his lips, but if he had slept, she did not see it in the strain of his brow, nor in the dark shadows underneath his eyes.

She took a brief moment to acknowledge that vulnerability before her eyes met his gaze. And then all she saw was the calculating brown, the victory gleam he disguised in his expression, but not in the lit depths.

He was *pleased* to surprise them—and to overhear a conversation never meant for him. But it was too early for any victories.

'I'm merely stating facts, Nicholas. Your need for adventure is no secret here. In fact, you made it very public when you left on one and never came back.'

'But my arriving now proves that I have returned.'

'It only proves that you're checking up on us. Isn't that why you were in the kitchens?'

'I was in the kitchens to see old and dear friends.'

'I think I see Mary,' Louve interjected.

She placed her hand on Louve's arm to hold him back. Under no circumstances would she let him escape. When he glanced at her he got the hint.

Turning to Nicholas, Louve asked, 'The kitchens, huh? How did Cook react?'

Nicholas glanced at her hand on Louve's arm. She'd meant to withdraw it, but in some small measure she took comfort at the simple contact, and she didn't want to withdraw it merely because Nicholas's gaze had suddenly darkened.

'As she always has.' Nicholas's voice was even, but not friendly. 'She gave me a thick slice of bread with an even thicker slab of butter before I even started my greeting.'

Matilda just stopped herself from digging her nails into Louve's arm. This exchange was ridiculous. Nicholas had returned to Mei Solis to meet some agenda, perhaps to insult them all and show his uncaring soul, not simply to be fed. How could she keep quiet with a man who did not mourn his friend and had never replied to their letters?

She bit her lip, trying not to retort, but her eyes strayed to the doors and she knew Nicholas was watching her.

Nicholas smirked. 'Would you prefer it if I left right now, instead of after the winter?'

He had heard every word.

Good.

Yet again she tried to hide her need to sweep past him and open the doors wide for him to step through. That would have been the old Matilda, the reckless one who had showed no caution. *That* Matilda had never served her well. Now, no matter how desperately she wanted Nicholas gone, a part of her wanted to be Roger's wife and the mother of his child. To be calm, to remember that they had all once been friends.

She didn't know Nicholas's reason for being here. Roger's death had been mere months ago, but Nicholas had given her no condolences nor apologised for not being here. Other than that time after his father's death, when he had became obsessed with repairing Mei Solis, he'd never shown any interest in his home or the rich fields surrounding it. And now he gave no clue to his motivation.

He held neither the boyish looks of his youth nor the easy open temperament. This man before her was a stranger. Dark gaze, even darker mien. She'd never been friends with *this* mercenary.

'Don't be foolish, Nicholas. You apparently need rest, and the weather will soon prevent you from leaving.'

'So you do show concern at my welfare? At my inability to ride because of travel weariness? Or are you afraid that I might catch cold?'

Louve almost choked on his ale. Nicholas ignored it. Matilda tapped Louve's arm. *Remember what Roger would want.*

'Of course we're concerned for your welfare, and we haven't had a chance to hear properly of your travels. This is your home.'

'Ah, yes, my *home*,' Nicholas said, his gaze roaming the hall. It was a brief relief from a gaze that always saw too much, before he narrowed it on her again. 'There's more than that that prevents me from leaving.'

A fissure of warning opened up inside her at those words. Most definitely he had some reason to be here, but it wasn't for Roger. No word of condolence, nor apology for not being here to bury him. It wasn't his home and it wasn't her.

Louve's arm tensed when she asked, 'What could that possibly be?'

The victory light in Nicholas's eye returned, and she knew she was the foolish one.

'I've returned with bags of silver to make Mei Solis everything you've ever wanted. You will have the ability to make repairs, purchase supplies for a thousand new roofs or new buildings. Or tear the whole thing down and start again.'

Simple words. Insulting words. Matilda's nails dug into Louve's arm before she could hide her response.

The look on Matilda's face was exactly what Nicholas had hoped for when he'd caught her and Louve unawares. The one she had denied him when she had turned away slowly to hide her response. She couldn't hide her response now, and he revelled in it.

Petty of him, he knew, but he'd once found some balance in his life and now he could find none. Even his quarters, which were meant to be his sanctuary, had haunted and mocked him. He'd reeled when he saw the rooms, the evidence of all Matilda had done. He hadn't been able to bark out his instructions to move elsewhere fast enough.

After a quick bath, he'd left to investigate the rear of Mei Solis and visit the kitchens. To greet Cook, with deeper furrows between her eyes from her frowns, and more around her mouth from her frequent smiles. It had been good to see her again.

However, not as satisfying as this. Having the

advantage and striding up to Matilda and Louve, who had been looking towards the stairs and not the servants' entrance. Reminding her who exactly she was. Someone greedier even than the woman who'd killed his father.

Mei Solis had been crumbling down, its roof collapsed. He'd ridden off to earn coin for their home—only to be shown that Matilda could spend his silver and have another man.

He'd dealt the verbal strike, but he'd felt a blow himself when her hand had tightened on Louve's arm. Another man...any man but him.

'When the light comes tomorrow we can show you what has been done,' Matilda said, her voice tight.

Still not good enough for him. 'So the work's all done and the coin I bring now is unnecessary? Perhaps I'll spend it on trivial matters. I notice my rooms need updating.'

Matilda paled, and Louve's hand grasped hers on his arm. Nicholas tracked their familiarity with each other.

'When has coin ever become unnecessary?'

Louve said, his voice light, though there was a dark warning in his eyes.

Nicholas was past warnings. It was time for him to give some of his own. 'True. It is convenient for bribes, debts, wars and weapons.'

'Mercenary work? Nothing we've seen here,' Louve said. 'I speak of boundary fences. The coin we've gained from the fields has supported this, but not soon enough. There are times when deer have been as destructive as the weather.'

'Boundary fences?'

Nicholas knew of enemies and boundaries— was all too aware of how they could be crossed. He had no interest in the stone and mortar kind, but still, an inspection would serve his purposes. Maybe he'd invite Roger to go with him, and there in the empty fields he'd demand his honour returned. If Roger ever showed.

Nicholas rolled his shoulders. Whatever sense of homecoming he'd felt in the kitchens was now gone. There was only the strain in his shoulders, the weight in his stance. The weight of this moment—as if this pause, this time, held some significance.

For what or for whom? A pregnant woman and a man who made too many jokes? If so, this was *his* welcome home feast and there was one guest missing.

'It's getting late, isn't it?' he said, turning his head towards Matilda.

'We should eat,' Matilda agreed.

'Surely the fields are empty at this time of year?' At their quizzical looks, he added, 'It's too late for man or beast to still be out.'

Matilda frowned. 'We've been able to get the work done before dark these last few years…'

That wasn't what he was asking. Over the years he'd received Louve's reports and, despite everything else, he trusted them when it came to maintaining the estate.

What and who he *didn't* trust was Roger, who was avoiding this welcoming feast. However, eventually Roger would be expected to enter the hall to eat. Until then…

'I will wait to sit until everyone is present.'

Nothing. Louve looked mildly curious while Matilda stayed implacable. Did they expect him to say nothing about the man—his friend—

who'd stabbed him in the heart? Then they didn't know him very well. He'd wait until next winter if that was what it took.

Louve drained his ale, the tenants' chatter eased, and all eyes turned to him. Of course they would—because they couldn't eat unless he sat. He wanted to announce that it wasn't he who delayed their meal, but a coward. One he should have faced years ago.

He had been travelling for weeks alone, lacking sleep in order to protect his horses and the satchels. His body ached and rest beckoned. Still he stood, waited, and thought about what he would say to Roger. His childhood friend, his reeve, who took care of the crops. Waited for the man who loved his betrothed but hadn't had the courtesy to tell him, who had married her and given her a child.

Patience, he told himself. But it wouldn't come. Not with all eyes turning to him now. Not with the constrictive band and the pressure of the patch over his eye. His right hand tightened as if it wanted to grasp a sword. His heart thumped as if he rode onto a field of enemies.

He'd been polite and had enquired gently regarding Roger's absence. He'd waited for Roger to reveal himself, or for Louve and Matilda to inform him of Roger's whereabouts. He'd come here to bury his past. To seek some revenge. To demand apologies. The man had married the woman he loved, and now he wouldn't show his face.

Enough was enough. Right now he would demand that Roger show himself. He wouldn't wait for answers—he'd force them.

He didn't—couldn't—ease his stance, or the tension mounting inside him as he bit out every word. 'Matilda, where is your husband?'

There was a sound from Louve and Matilda paled. The crowd around them faded. The lights seemed to dim as her brows drew in.

No. No balance. No patience. No understanding.

His fingers curled and there was a roaring in his ears as he glanced to Louve, whose expression was stricken, his mouth slack.

Nicholas glanced behind them to the Great Doors that remained shut, and the tenants waiting by their seats. Even the children and the animals were finding their places.

There wasn't space for anyone else.

His gaze locked on Matilda. There was a flush in her cheeks and an answering emotion gleaming in her hazel eyes. He recognised them all. Anger. Rage. A warrior's cry for battle.

His sense of betrayal was overwhelming. Patience? Balance? None to be found. He shook his head—a warning to himself, to Louve, who stood agape. To Matilda, whose lips had parted.

He was lifting his curling fist before she said the words, 'He's dead.'

Nicholas struck.

Chapter Four

'You should go after him,' Louve said, holding his sleeve to his bloodied lip.

Matilda crouched beside her fallen friend. Louve had hit the floor faster than she had been able to react to what Nicholas had done. The corner of his lip was bleeding and the entire right side of his face was bright red, his eyelid beginning to swell.

'Your eye!'

'He only glanced it. I'm lucky.'

'Lucky? *Lucky* is being told that Cook didn't burn all the bread for the day. The right side of your face is swelling faster than said bread loaves is *not* Fortune smiling on you.'

Her heart would not stop thumping and her every word shook. That moment when Nicholas swung. The expression on Nicholas's face. Something raw, visceral. It had gone through her before she'd registered what he meant to do.

Louve had been completely unprepared.

The people in the hall had been unprepared too, as the crack of Nicholas's fist against Louve's jaw had reverberated against the stone.

She hadn't heard Louve hitting the ground— not through the sudden gasps of the crowd.

Then there had been a void of sound, except for Nicholas's harsh breaths and his brutal growl aimed at no one as he stormed through the unnaturally still room and out through the Great Doors.

'Lucky?' she repeated. 'You're bleeding. And despite him only glancing it, you'll have a black eye.'

'Luckier yet, for Mary will care for me now.'

Matilda saw Mary, standing as still as the rest of the crowd. She'd never understand the hold she had over her friend. 'You're incorrigible.'

Louve took her hands and helped her stand. Then he waved off the now circling crowd with a smile. The crowd dispersed, but the chatter increased. Soon everyone within a day's ride would know of what had happened here tonight.

What a great welcome from the lord of Mei Solis. No, it had been a welcome from a mercenary. Nicholas had always been impulsive, but that violence hadn't come from the Nicholas she'd once known.

'You should go after him,' Louve told her.

'You're the one he struck—don't you want to talk to him?'

'Not this time.' Louve flexed his hand and gave her a look she recognised from years of friendship. 'I dare you.'

'That won't work on me.' And no such childish challenge would influence the mercenary who had strode out of the Great Hall. 'Nicholas has gone, and maybe he'll keep on going.'

'You know where he went. And, despite his aim, it's you he needs to talk to. He's been gone a long time, but from his reaction...' Louve placed his hand on her arm. 'He didn't know about Roger, Matilda. You can't leave him like that.'

She could. 'He *left* us.'

'He's returned to find his friend dead. Not only

a friend, but *Roger*. For all he knows, Roger could have been gone for years.'

'The time of Roger's passing makes no difference. Nicholas chose his path years ago—as I chose mine. He left first. He holds no more importance to Roger's death than to any other friend. In truth…' In truth she saw little of the man she had once called her betrothed. 'You don't know if he thinks of *any* of us as a friend. He never answered our letters.'

'You think he feels nothing over Roger's death? He struck me in his home—in front of his people. That's some indication of where his heart is.'

She didn't want to think of Nicholas's heart. He didn't deserve it. Yet Roger had been her friend and her husband. And in that she knew she was the one to answer whatever questions Nicholas might have.

Dares didn't work, but she always faced her challenges.

She knew the path towards the chapel's graveyard all too well. Her mother and her husband were buried here, and she visited them every day. However, instead of taking the well-worn path she turned left towards the other side. The one that wasn't lit by the villagers' fires and lanterns, but only by moonlight and stars.

Still, she could see Nicholas—exactly where Louve had said he'd be. No statue or grave marker, no matter how grand, was as dark or forbidding as the man towering amongst them.

Two hands gripped a statue's base, and his head was bowed between his arms. To anyone else he'd look to be praying next to his father's grave. However, his father was buried inside, under the chapel's great stones, not outside, battered by the elements.

It could be freezing here at night, with nothing to buffer against the wind. Nicholas, bent against his father's memorial, looked like a man braving harsh weather. To her, he looked like a man shoving a broken plough through rocky ground.

'You shouldn't have come here.' Nicholas's resonating voice, tinged with pain, reverberated across the cold stones.

Refusing to feel pity, she ignored his grief. Still... 'We sent you a message.'

He raised his head, but did not stop gripping

the statue's base. As if he held it up...or maybe it supported him. Whatever the reason, the tightness of his hands was visible to her, but not his expression. It took a moment longer for her eyes to adjust and then she realised it wasn't only the darkness making his gaze unreadable...it was something of himself that was unknown to her as well.

'I don't want to talk of Roger,' he said.

Conflicting emotions seemed to be battering him. There was pain there, and anger, confusion and something else. She ignored all that at his words. There was only one reason he didn't want to talk about Roger. Because he didn't care.

'Of course you don't.'

'Your meaning...?'

'You don't deserve to know my meaning.'

He pushed himself off the statue and rose to his full height. His will seemed to reach out to her and she brushed it aside.

Turning away, she said, 'It seems colder here than anywhere else.'

She only made a few steps before he said, 'How many more are there?'

Ignoring him, she took a few more steps. Her reason for coming out here was to talk of Roger, but Nicholas had made it clear that wasn't what he wanted.

His standing next to his father's memorial and not the new headstone of his friend should have been an indication of how futile her coming here was. He obviously still worshiped his father's desires above anyone else's...even his own.

Or maybe she had never really known what Nicholas's desires were. She'd always argued that he followed his father's desires and never his own. Maybe his desires *were* his father's, and it was she who was blind.

It was an old argument, and one that she'd thought was put to rest after she'd married Roger. It should have been put to rest—and yet here she was walking through the night to face him again. It hadn't yet been a full day into his return.

Another step away, and still Nicholas's gaze collided against her. She ignored him, but couldn't ignore her own curiosity. What did he mean by how many? How many deaths?

Biting back a sound of frustration, she pivoted to face him. 'How many what?'

Nicholas was only a few steps away. She hadn't heard him following her and wasn't prepared for him to be so close.

It didn't matter that it was only moonlight illuminating them because he was no longer in the monument's shadows. So when she turned she surprised him, and glimpsed his expression before he shuttered it.

'How many other children, Matilda?' he asked.

There was a whirling darkness in his gaze, a furrow between his brow. His shoulders hunched as if he'd taken a fist to his guts. She'd thought the emotion gone before he'd uttered his question, but it wasn't. He was in *agony*.

His pain had to be feigned. For the last three years his correspondence had been only perfunctory and infrequent. He had never enquired about his tenants or his friends.

He had never answered her letter to him.

Trying to gain distance, she wrapped her arms around her stomach and watched his lids flutter closed for a moment, as if her action affected him. She wouldn't let him affect *her*.

'You want to talk of my baby?' She wanted to shout. 'Are you concerned that a widow with children will deplete Mei Solis resources? Or, more precisely, that I won't be able to do my duties as bailiff? That your linens won't be clean enough or I won't be able to settle disputes for you?'

The wind buffeted them, but his words pounded against her. 'Isn't it *you* who is concerned with linens and the depletion of precious Mei Solis resources?'

Like some spoiled, selfish shrew? Not her. She wasn't his stepmother, Helena. She'd begged him to stay, to tear down Mei Solis and live a simpler life. Instead he'd left to bring more riches, making it very clear to her what he deemed important. So she had married another.

And yet he accused her of this?

'After all these years...' She only just held back the urge to kick him. 'This is what you want to say to me?'

Nicholas opened his mouth. Closed it. And she felt the satisfaction in that.

Until he said, 'Does it feel like I've been gone years?'

His voice was low, contemplative. She knew immediately how to respond to the judgemental, accusing Nicholas, but not to this man. Rubbing her arms against the wind, ignoring his steady gaze, she gave his answer some thought.

How long did it feel? Like centuries and like just yesterday. Especially since he'd brought up everything from the past simply by returning. It didn't matter how much time, it mattered what was felt.

And she shouldn't be feeling *anything* for him. No matter what his presence here meant. She'd married another. Loved and grieved for another and was now carrying his child.

'Your absence has no bearing on what I feel. You were gone six years and that's the truth. What we care for or feel matters not.'

'I care very much.'

Judgement, accusation, and now lies. 'For what?

In three years I have heard nothing from you, and you're here now—'

'I'm here now because this is my home.'

More lies. 'Don't give me sentiment. This property is your *income*.'

There was a curve to his lips, but his fingers flexed as if to release tension. 'It is my home.'

Which didn't give him the right simply to return and order them around. She bent and scraped some of the almost solid soil into her palm. When she stood again, she tossed it at him. '*This* is yours—the rest of us are not.'

He suddenly became as dark as the soil still clinging to her fingers. 'You made sure of that.'

'I?' She brushed the soil off, desperate to remove all traces of his property from her body. She wanted no part of any of this. 'I had nothing to do with your leaving *or* your staying away.'

'You had everything to do with it.' He took a step forward, leaning towards her as if he meant to plough her down. His *queue* was loose, his hair whipping in the wind. 'Everything! You who—'

He didn't say any more, but she'd heard enough.

A mere day since he'd returned, their first conversation, and it was nothing but barbs and jabs and not anything she could possibly understand, even though she had been a part of it all.

Except… She'd made promises that weren't part of what had been between Nicholas and her.

She'd made vows to love and marry Roger. To raise their child as he would want. They'd talked about when Nicholas returned and if it would matter. She'd told her husband that it wouldn't, because she wanted a new life. Or at least to look at the one she had differently. She'd made her choice and so had Nicholas. Still, it had hurt Roger when Nicholas had never replied, but he'd forgiven him.

She thought she'd forgiven him, too. Yet, here she was with him in a graveyard at night. She was supposed to have changed, but turmoil roiled inside her. Anything between them was supposed to be dead.

'And you're here now expecting what?' She gestured at him, at their surroundings.

'Answers!' He pulled himself away then, as

if he hadn't meant to say that word or put any emphasis on it.

Answers. In that she would agree—it was why she had written to him.

'Then you should have replied to my letter.'

He hadn't because he didn't truly want answers. He was a mercenary—had fashioned himself to be a trained killer. He'd wanted to leave this home that she loved, and he'd wanted never to return. Now he made demands for no reason.

'Your letter?' His expression turned mutinous. 'Damn your letter. How could I have answered that? Do you know when I *received* your precious letter?'

His hand went to the back of his head, as if to brush through his hair, but his fingers stopped at the strap of the eye patch.

Biting out another curse, he jerked his hand away before locking his venomous gaze with her. 'Too. Late. *That's* when I received your letter.'

Nicholas was like a berserker, crying for blood across the field, and everything in her wanted to answer. To raise her own sword and strike the killing blow.

He was a madman, a mercenary with no conscience. He should be mourning his friend's death. Should be apologising for not answering their letters. He should have been here when her mother died.

He'd done nothing.

And Louve had sent her out here to provide comfort. There was no comforting madness and cruelty.

They stood here in this graveyard, shouting on matters that had no bearing in the present. Right now it wasn't about them, or the past and their arguments. Those had been long decided by his absence, by his deeds. All that mattered now was that she was the one who'd married Roger; she had been there at his death. And she'd go to her grave making sure that Nicholas, who had abandoned them all, knew why.

'Stop making this into something it's not. You don't care about what happened to us. Roger's dead. And I refuse to let you ignore that.'

He huffed out a breath as if she had hit him. 'I'm not ignoring his death.'

A strike to Louve's jaw…standing in the night surrounded by graves… Maybe he wasn't ignoring Roger's death, but he wasn't acknowledging it either.

'You refuse to talk about him.'

'It's pointless.'

The pain in her belly was so sharp she was certain it was physical. 'Pointless?' she gasped as she locked gazes with him.

There was so much there in his face as his brows drew in, as his lips parted. He wanted to say something, but then his face shut down again. The hard angles of his jaw, the slash of his cheekbones. The strip of leather along his left cheek. His scar. His eye. Why did she see it now, and not when he'd struck Louve, or when he'd gripped his father's memorial?

To see beyond his injury must be a weakness in her. For it was the wound of a man who killed for a living. She must remember to look at that silvery bisecting jaggedness to remind her that this man had no heart.

'You're right,' she said. 'It *is* pointless. Louve told me to come here and tell you, and you don't care.'

'Not now. Not yet.' His words were clipped, as if he'd forced them out.

'Is this too soon?' she mocked. 'Did you want to wait a few days? Get some rest? Have Cook prepare huge meals?'

'It is too soon for this.'

'Because today you returned? If you didn't want to hear any of this you could have kept away—like the coward you are.'

'Coward?' he growled. 'You want to hear what I want to know? I want to know if that child you bear is even Roger's. Or is it Louve's?'

Something colder than ice sliced through her. 'Louve's?'

He waved his arm. 'He was standing by you so protectively this evening. Roger isn't here. What am I to guess?'

What was he to *guess*? He should have *known*. Known never to accuse her of going from him, to Roger, to Louve. She could hate him in this moment.

'You've changed.'

He gave a mocking exhalation. 'Not enough.'

Too much. So easily she could hate him. So easily she could turn the shame and the sting to her pride when he'd left her begging into something darker and more bitter. Turn the emotions into being more like him. A mad mercenary.

Everything about Nicholas was as sharp as a sword. Bitter. Cold. Hurting.

And yet agony was there in his voice. Everything in her fought to acknowledge it, yet she couldn't when the heart of his question was more significant than her pride. In a way, without asking about Roger, he *was*.

'You need to know,' she said.

'I don't,' he mocked. 'But you'll tell me anyway, won't you?'

She wanted to throw more dirt at him and walk away, but she'd changed since he'd left. She could face his anger…and his agony. For Roger's sake, she'd force him to listen to her.

'This child is Roger's, Nicholas,' she said. 'He died mere weeks ago, knowing he'd be a father.'

Nicholas shook his head—once, twice. Then

he pivoted suddenly, took a step away from her, then another. His shoulders rose and fell with great gusts of breath.

She waited, but he remained silent and didn't turn again. He didn't walk away. Maybe he knew if he did, it would be she who silently followed him on this graveyard path. She who would stand close so that when he turned he'd be surprised.

She would be cleverer than him and let none of her emotions show. With his back turned, she could tell nothing of what he felt now, but she didn't care. He stood still, and for Roger's sake she'd make sure Nicholas heard every word.

'Roger died by a scythe wielded by a mere child who, though it was not his fault, carries great remorse. He was training the children as he used to. It was only a cut, and yet it wouldn't heal. It wouldn't heal and he *died*. Yet here you are, asking about my children, and what burden they'll mean for your *estate*.' She forced this last word through her constricted throat.

Roger's death had been senseless and horrific. He'd been in such pain, and utterly incoherent as his leg turned black. Death's pungent odour had filled their home and blanketed the cradle newly built for their child.

When his condition had worsened she'd feared for Roger, felt the grief of knowing he would never see their child, would never grow old with her.

In the end even that sweet, painful grief had been obliterated by Roger's sudden shouts, his babbling words, the mocking pus that had oozed from the festering wound. And then had come the bitter remembrance of the healer's words, that Matilda should have severed the leg when she'd told her to. Nonetheless, she'd thought…

Nicholas turned. The moonlight played tricks, making the man before her seem suddenly like the man who had left six years ago. However, *this* Nicholas had declared knowing about his friend's death was pointless. He'd told her the child she carried was a burden. She had thought she'd hated him all those years ago, when he'd stopped answering her letters, when he'd decided to continue his mercenary life, but it was nothing to how she felt now.

'I'm asking about your children because—' he began.

'No!' She could hold her turmoil for Roger's sake, but she wouldn't allow him to insult her baby again. 'You will not talk about my children. You *left* me—your friends, your home.' Her voice broke. 'At the end Roger called for you. Shouted your name. And you say knowing how he died is pointless! Who do you think you are? Why have you bothered to return?'

He gave her nothing but an open stare that told her nothing. Disgusted with herself for her outburst, and with him for his lack of compassion, she turned and hurried her steps away.

She was faster this time, and was almost around the chapel when the wind that battered against them carried words she shouldn't have heard.

'I don't know.'

Chapter Five

It was almost midday when Agnes skipped towards Matilda as she and Bess passed her home.

The sun had barely broken before Bess had knocked on her door to tell her what had happened after she and Nicholas had left the hall. So lost had she been in her confrontation with Nicholas in the graveyard, Matilda had forgotten about Louve, the tenants, and the great welcoming feast.

Apparently, Louve had laughed about the incident. He'd announced to everyone that he'd dared Nicholas's fist and had been too slow to duck properly. Bess had reported that everyone had enjoyed the feast, but the whispers hadn't stopped until Louve had addressed the entire hall and made it into a game: *Guess what I dared the Lord of Mei Solis...*

When she'd asked Bess what some of them had guessed, Bess had been silent. One look at her expression and Matilda had known she didn't want the answer.

She took Agnes's hand.

Out of the corner of her eye she saw two males with equal stride walking another path; but when she turned her head they were gone. Could it have been Nicholas and Louve? Or just a memory of them walking together?

She felt a yank on her arm, and she laughed at Agnes's restless feet. 'I'm not skipping today!'

'You never skip.'

'I *always* skip, but the baby hasn't learned how to yet.'

Agnes immediately stilled. 'Can I teach her?'

'When she can use her own two legs.'

Agnes's grin grew, and Matilda's heart eased. Agnes's enthusiasm for everything was infectious. At eight years old, and with four older brothers, Agnes often sought Matilda for play.

'If you're settled, I'm getting back to my own home,' Bess said.

Matilda nodded. Bess gave her a warning look before waving them off. Matilda knew she'd have to tell Bess something about her conversation with Nicholas. She just didn't know what.

Nicholas's vehement response to the subject of her letter? His lack of apology? How he hadn't wanted to know of Roger's death, but only of how many burdens she'd bred in the time since he went away…and had they been by multiple men?

Six years… She'd imagined their first conversation as something polite, from a distance. After all, he'd broken their betrothal because he hadn't wanted it any more, and she'd married Roger.

Nothing between them last night had been polite. Instead they'd shouted their emotions at each other. She felt every jab. Six years… And in one night he had made her feel exposed, *vulnerable*.

She stumbled, grabbed at her skirts with her free hand and nodded to Agnes, who forged ahead again so that Matilda felt every tug of the child's exuberance.

And that was what she'd seen when she'd turned. Before he had been able to hide his thoughts. Nicholas had been *vulnerable*. It seemed impossible, but it was absolutely unmistakable even in the broad light of day.

No discourse, only emotions. They'd been themselves to each other. But how could she tell any of that to Bess? It had all been too personal. Even the night and the wind's swirling belonged to no one else.

There was a clench to her heart, a bend to the path, and she slowed her steps. Nothing belonged to *them*.

Afraid her suddenly weak legs would crash beneath her, Matilda begged Agnes to stop.

'Did I hurt her?' Agnes studied Matilda's belly.

Matilda patted her stomach. 'Not possible. She's hardy enough.'

'I wish *I* was stronger.'

Ah. This was familiar ground. 'What did your brothers do today?'

Agnes's lip stuck out briefly. 'Peter hid my stockings, which were hanging near the fire.'

Matilda gave a quick glance to the child's legs. 'It looks like you found them.'

'They were hanging outside.'

Oh. Damp instead of dry and warm.

'Some time today, find every pair of braies Peter has and get them to me as soon as possible.'

Agnes's eyes widened. 'Ooh, what'll you do?'

Matilda winked. 'You'll see.'

Something of Agnes's predicament in having four brothers always brought out Matilda's more mischievous side. Maybe it was the fact that her closest friends were boys which made her a kindred spirit with the child. Oh, she'd never do anything cruel—just teach Peter a lesson, as she'd used to do with—

A heaviness sank her heart. She had only one friend now. Not everything was the same as in the past. Nicholas and Louve wouldn't have been out walking together earlier. Not after Nicholas had struck Louve in front of everyone.

Louve was still her friend, and she was grateful for the sacrifices he made last night, but she knew he'd paid the price.

Too handsome for his own good, and too talented at everything he started, there had always been a part of Louve that felt he didn't deserve his good fortune. Why he should feel like that, she didn't know, and in order to keep their friendship she'd never asked, but Nicholas striking him in front of all his friends had been a great insult.

And Louve, by saying he'd deserved it, had made it worse for himself. However, he'd done it to keep the peace. To ensure everyone ate the food Cook had so painstakingly made. He was truly her friend, and Matilda meant to keep that friendship. That wouldn't be happening if she did anything the way the old Matilda had. The old Matilda and her pranks had driven everyone away.

Resigned to this, she said, 'Agnes, maybe you *shouldn't* hand me Peter's braies. Maybe Peter only did that to your stockings to gain your attention. Hasn't he ever pulled your plait only to laugh and hug you?'

'Maybe...' the child said hesitantly, and Matilda knew she had it right. Roger would have wanted Agnes to treat vindictiveness with kindness.

'Maybe Peter was simply showing you affection. Maybe he doesn't understand how uncomfortable it is to put on damp clothes. You should try and forgive him.'

'How am I to do that?'

The boy was older, bigger, and far too rough. His antics were often cruel. Stealing his sister's stockings was almost nice in comparison to his past actions. 'Perhaps play with him?'

Agnes scrunched her nose.

It was a terrible idea. The boy truly needed to be taught a lesson. But it shouldn't be coming from Matilda and her own foolish sense fairness.

'It's worth a try,' she said weakly.

The light in Agnes's eyes dimmed, but she shrugged.

Matilda wanted to offer better words of wisdom, but having an even temperament and doing the right thing still didn't come easily to her, no matter what lessons she'd learned or how badly she wanted to change. All she could do was squeeze Agnes's hand and feel her matching response. Matilda feared she took more comfort than she gave, but the child didn't seem to mind.

Another turn in the road brought new sights and sounds of the village. There was Rohesia, the healer, waving a spoon and shouting at Matilda's father for standing too close to the fire.

Matilda hurried her steps and her legs protested at the extra stretch. It was worse today. She felt a hitch that wouldn't allow her to move. She'd need to hide it or someone would confine her earlier than she wanted. Simply the thought of staying within four walls made her heart stutter.

Eyeing her father's bewildered expression, and Rohesia's belligerent one, she slowed her steps. 'Agnes, you can return to your home. I'll see you in a bit.'

'Are we building today?'

Agnes always wanted to build and create. Why she continually asked *her*, she didn't know, but at some point Agnes had started asking her to draw in the dirt and build with her. The day was early, but Matilda knew there would be no spare time later.

But Agnes was a child, with a child's understanding of the passing of the day. 'Maybe tomorrow.'

Agnes frowned.

Matilda stopped walking until the little girl looked at her. Out of the corner of her eye she saw her father's growing agitation. 'I'll truly try tomorrow. I promise.'

Agnes, her focus now on Rohesia and Matilda's father, seemed to make a decision, and then she quickly turned and ran.

Exhaling, Matilda walked closer to the familiar crisis taking place. Neither party acknowledged her. Rohesia's confrontations with her father were never easy, but her father's agitation made matters much worse.

'Father.' No response. 'Holgar.'

There was a turning of his head, even as his fingers fumbled with his breeches' laces. No doubt he was about to urinate upon the embers and put out the fire. Since Roger's death he'd started doing this. No one knew why, or how to stop him. She didn't want to see him hurt, but it seemed inevitable. It would happen either by Rohesia's ladle, or by the fire's flames licking at his ballocks.

She put her hand on his arm, which stilled him. 'Rohesia's cooking. See—that's her food, and she needs the fire to cook it.'

'He'll be ruining my bread again!' said Rohesia.

Matilda winced. The bread was nestled in the flames. If her father kept his aim it *would* be ruined.

Rohesia was just as old as her father. Yet where her father had always been a gentle soul, Rohesia was as short-tempered as a snake and just as quick to strike. No matter how fragile her father was, the old healer would use the ladle.

She should know. Rohesia's ladles had been used on *her* for as long as she could remember.

'He won't ruin your bread.' She addressed her father. 'You won't, will you?'

'I like bread,' he said, his eyes on her.

'I know you do. So, all you have to do is step back and wait a bit.'

'There's a fire,' he said.

'That's because of the bread. Just a few moments more, then you can eat.'

Though Rohesia didn't lower her ladle, Matilda exhaled in relief as her father secured the last lace and sat where she indicated. She'd take her victories where she could.

'He'll be fine now,' she told Rohesia.

'Your father is getting worse.'

'He's not,' she said, though she had her doubts.

Many people cared for her father at Mei Solis, and she and Roger had shared their grain with different families in payment for such help. Since her father's home was next to Rohesia's, Matilda gave not grain, but the finest of flours to the old healer.

Nevertheless, Rohesia couldn't watch him every moment. And neither could she. It had been easier when Roger was around, but— Matilda put her hand to her belly. It was inevitable. At some point her father would truly hurt himself and no one would be able to help him.

'I can make him more tea,' Rohesia groused. 'It seems to help.'

'Thank you.' The offer of help was merely temporary, but she'd take it. Rohesia cared—even if her manner was gruff.

Rohesia pointed her ladle at Matilda. 'You've done too much today.'

'And there's more to do.'

'I suspect because the Lord's returned?'

Matilda nodded, not about to confess that most of her work was in trying to comprehend her muddled and twisted thoughts about Nicholas in the graveyard. 'I'm having trouble moving my legs today. They're hitching.'

Glancing at Holgar, who was still staring at the fire, Rohesia hobbled over to Matilda and grabbed her hips with gnarled hands. 'It's too early for this.'

'For what?'

Lowering her voice, Rohesia said, 'Your hips get loose before you birth.' She frowned. 'You've weeks to go.'

'Will the baby be all right?'

'Baby's fine. You...not so good.'

Suddenly unsteady, Matilda sat down next to her father. She'd wanted a child for as long as she could remember. She and Roger had expected one from the first year of their marriage. Three years on and they'd almost lost hope. With Roger gone, this baby was her *only* hope. Was Rohesia now saying that her baby would be without *any* parent?

Her vision blurring with tears, she gasped out, 'What's wrong with me?'

Rohesia scoffed, returned to her bread and flipped it. 'You'll live, but you need rest. Go slower.'

Blinking, she stated, 'I'm already slow.'

'Slower. If you don't, you'll lose the babe.' Rohesia's shrug belied her serious tone. 'You won't have much choice. If your hips hitch you'll barely be walking.'

She was worried for herself and her baby, but she had other worries too. 'How will I go to the fields, the home and manor?'

'Worry about that when the time comes. You have other more prominent worries, no?'

'Other than dinner—'

'There's the man who has returned as well.'

This argument again. One she didn't want to

hear or for others to overhear. 'I made my decision.'

Rohesia had a calculating look in her eye as she looked pointedly at Holgar. 'Or was it made for you?'

Her father was clasping and unclasping his hands. She had thought him lost to his thoughts, but now she wondered how much he understood. He hadn't liked Nicholas's leaving. His grief when her mother had died had been immense, and then he'd pleaded with her to accept Roger's offer.

His wishes had been emotional, nonetheless his reasoning had been sound, since she had known Roger long before Nicholas had left Mei Solis or her mother had died. It had seemed rational for her to marry Roger.

'What do you mean by that?' she asked.

Rohesia turned her attention to the pot of soup on the fire. 'Not my place—never has been.'

The old healer hadn't a humble bone in her twisted back.

Matilda stood. 'I've rested enough. I need to check on the evening meal.'

'You'll be going slow?'

'I will.'

Without this baby… She didn't want to think of what she had already lost.

'Where the hell are we walking to?' Nicholas asked after they'd made their way through the village and were more than halfway through his demesne fields.

'Just to the fields,' Louve replied.

Louve walked on Nicholas's left, and couldn't see the bruising on Louve's face, but the tenants could, and they eyed the two men, most likely expecting another confrontation. It had been down to their watchful gaze, rather than Louve's request or his battered face, that Nicholas had agreed to follow him. However, they were beyond the tenants' stares now, and he expected answers.

'We're *in* the fields,' he pointed out.

'The outer ones,' Louve said, just as quickly.

The ones he'd ridden through yesterday. Fallow fields that were full of rocks. Nothing else.

Louve continued to stare ahead. His gait was

comfortable, at ease. He hadn't demanded an apology, and he didn't act as if he expected Nicholas to offer him one. This had all the makings of an aimless jaunt, but Louve wasn't talking. And he always talked.

This wasn't what Nicholas had expected when he'd woken that morning. Woken? He'd never gone to sleep. Lying in a bed, in a part of his home he'd never before slept in, he had found no answers to his questions.

There wasn't a solution. Roger was dead and his thoughts had simply swung back and forth like a dangling dagger. And he'd waited all night for it to drop.

He didn't know how to repair the past when revenge and demands for honour had been his only plan. Now, with Roger's death, even that was impossible. His raw anger at Matilda last night showed how futile any conversation with her would be. He couldn't maintain his reasoning around her. Not with the way he felt…not with her carrying a child that wasn't his.

So what was left for him?

No sleep, no solution… But he could at least

find distraction, and that was why he had welcomed Louve's approach in the courtyard. The man's easy expression had been marred by a swollen lip and a bruised eye, but he had recommended a trip to the fields.

It was as good as distraction as any, and yet… 'There's nothing in those fields.'

'That's the point.'

There was no point—unless Louve wanted a true fight. Maybe one part of his past could be repaired. Maybe he could still demand satisfaction.

'I didn't bring my sword.'

There was a huff from Louve, as if he wanted to laugh. 'I've prepared what we need.'

This was familiar ground. To train, to fight—all the things he'd done for the last six years. 'You think to even the score? You *deserved* my fist.'

'If you believe so.' Louve pointed to the largest unmarked field, which now held two sets of oxen and ploughs. 'Nevertheless, *you* deserve this.'

They were almost an apparition. They'd had two oxen when Nicholas had left, and that had been after years of back-breaking work. Now there was two sets of four, and ploughs and blades substantial enough to withstand their strength.

He should be pleased by the difference, but there was nothing here except two men and two teams of oxen. Was it his years as a mercenary that had made him believe that matters could only be settled by the clashing of blades?

Or was this Louve's way of showing his displeasure at his return, at that thrown punch? Did Louve remember how much he hated this land and everything it represented? Of course he did.

'No swords, then.'

Louve shrugged. 'The ploughs have blades.'

This was no settling of differences. This was creating more.

'I never worked the farm before I left.'

He'd done carpentry on the manor and in the village houses. He'd dug ditches for the tanners and for waste. He'd trained and done his sums. The fields, the land—that was something he had left to Roger even then, and it made him less likely to touch them now. He'd wanted distraction from Roger, and how he'd cheated him of a wife and a future.

'What makes you think I'd do it now?'

Louve turned so his battered jaw was on full display. 'No reason.'

Nicholas refused to feel guilt, though striking Louve hadn't been his usual way. He never struck in anger—never killed without purpose. His fist cracking Louve's jaw had been senseless. His training as a knight, as a mercenary, had been abandoned in one blinding strike.

And Louve hadn't been his target. It had been a strike at Fate and just as useless. Last night he'd been blinded more than when he'd lost his eye. He'd been blinded by Roger's death, by Mei Solis, with its repairs shining brighter than ever, by Matilda's pregnancy, by being thwarted in his vengeance. In his quest for peace. He had no purpose here at all.

He turned to leave.

Louve exhaled roughly. 'I know why you struck me and so do you. Because you can't strike out at a man who's dead and you can't do anything to a pregnant woman.'

Nicholas stopped, looked to the ground and then answered. 'So you bring me here to do something I hate, which won't solve the question of why your jaw is prettier than it's ever been? To till a fallow field that won't feed anyone for years?'

He kicked at the soil, revealing the dark, fertile dirt between the rocks. Too many rocks, mocking the need for more land and crops.

'There's two teams of four now, and four more to divide amongst the tenants. Your demesne is already ploughed, and the tenants are using the other oxen and horses for theirs. This is all that's left.'

'You talk to me of *fields*?'

'It doesn't appear that you want to talk of the other matter.'

Roger and these fields were one and the same thing. He'd wanted distraction. This was shoving it in his face. 'She told you.'

'*You* told me, and now I can't see out of my eye.'

Nicholas wanted to growl. He'd gained no answers from Matilda in the graveyard, found no solace in Roger's death. And now it was just him and Louve and eight oxen, which pawed the dirt and huffed their impatience. Each team was restless. If they didn't take the reins soon they'd plough this untilled soil anyway. Eight beasts, vying for control, against him and against each other.

He eyed Louve, who was looking around him as if he had time to waste, to wait.

'Repair your past,' Rhain had urged.

It had meant returning here. He should have been prepared. Six years away, and he'd travelled far. Had seen and understood how others lived. Not everyone lived or wanted to live the way his family desired.

He'd fought and barely survived. He now understood the preciousness of life. He'd gained friendships outside of his home. Because of his injury, he'd gained insight. Now saw the best and worst of humanity.

But this place… It was as if no time had passed at all. And all his arguments, rage and frustration hadn't been resolved. And now he knew why. It wasn't just Mei Solis and his father's untimely death, or Helena. It was his three friends, so close they were like family. He'd trusted his home to them—his future, his soul. And then he had been betrayed. *My Soulless.*

It was fitting that he stood now in a fallow field. Its absolute desolation reflected his years away. He'd left trying to gain, and he had lost everything.

He should have brought his sword. Out here, he could swing it at nothing until he was exhausted. Instead, like a fool, he'd followed someone who wasn't his friend, to plough some field that would yield nothing but the misery of reflection.

'You're right. I don't want to talk.'

The teams stamped on the ground, their great heads shaking to loosen their shackles. Nicholas swept over to take the reins. He yanked on the leather and the oxen yanked back. Something reared inside him, and Nicholas welcomed the fight.

'Let's do this.'

'This is how you will begin? With no direction or instruction?' Louve stepped towards his own team. 'Have you been ploughing fields since you left? Ensuring each seed is planted carefully in a row? I'll tell you true—I'm looking forward to seeing the crooked rows you'll carve.'

Nicholas preferred facing his enemy on a battle field versus the machinations inside any fine manor house. And yet something inside him fell into place. He'd had no sleep and was restless. This wasn't a test with swords, but it was a challenge nonetheless. He recognised it in the light that lit Louve's eyes.

'You know what I've been doing,' Nicholas said. 'I haven't been swinging sickles or scythes at helpless stalks of wheat and barley all these years. I've been swinging swords towards men whose sole purpose was to kill me. I lost my eye and six years of my life to send you coin so you could have these oxen and these new ploughs.'

'Not for me. For Roger. His rows were so straight a blind man wouldn't stumble.'

'Damn you!'

The oxen surged forward and this time Nicholas didn't pull back, but urged them on to catch Louve by surprise and take the lead. When

Louve drove his oxen in the opposite direction, Nicholas kept his focus on remaining ahead.

Around and around they went. In opposite directions so that with each complete circle they met again. Three times, and Nicholas was fighting to keep his oxen straight. Though he was strong, he was out of practice—which only drove him faster, harder. Proving himself as he hadn't in years. The calluses on his hands would protect him from blisters, but not at this intensity. He welcomed the sting.

Another bend and this time, despite the cold wind, Louve's face was red with sweat. 'Ready to exchange words *now*, Mercenary?'

Nicholas held his oxen back just enough for him to reply. 'About a dead man and a pregnant woman?'

Louve flinched.

His words were coarse, but justified. Just like tilling this field, or returning here, nothing could be made whole again. 'Why task my strength on wasted endeavours?'

Louve looked as if he wanted to make first strike. 'Wasted? You've lost more than your eye fighting for coin. You never would have said that of your friends before. At one point we were family. In returning here, I thought that was what you wanted again.'

That was all he'd wanted, but it wasn't here. He'd lost everything. His life. His love. His friendship. And now, with his return, he'd lost his revenge. He hadn't set anything to rights, had allowed Roger to marry his betrothed. And Louve had stolen her away as surely as the other man. There would be no honour between them. There were no repairs for this and he didn't want them. This man had no honour.

'If you *were* family, you were as useless as this field.'

Louve pulled roughly on a rein. 'Is that what you want? For me to strike you back?'

Gladly. 'As if you could.'

'And yet you till this field with me?'

'I don't till a field with a man for a promise of friendship he has no intention of keeping. I'm here to keep from being badgered with useless chatter.'

Nicholas snapped the reins and the oxen surged

forward again. Another turn, but he'd get no peace. He could see Louve driving his oxen, driving them forward so their teams would meet again.

'Are you implying your rage is with *me*?' Louve shouted before he stopped his team.

'Yes!' Nicholas forced the word through the last of his breath, through the last of his strength, through the last of his beating heart. 'Without any doubt.'

Louve scowled. 'Is your need for coin that great? Is that what kept you away? Mei Solis is more prosperous than ever, and it's *not* because of the damn coin you sent. It's because I ensured the coin went far. Because Roger, Matilda—'

'Do you think I fault your stewardship? I sent you messages these years. In any of them, did I criticise your decisions?'

Nicholas had kept up his correspondence with Louve because he was his steward. Those letters had been safe, and any enemy would expect them since all lords kept track of their property. If he had cut out all correspondence, and he had been watched, as he'd suspected, that would have caused more suspicion.

'Then what?'

Revenge, answers, apologies from all three... That was all he needed to keep the promise he'd made to Rhain. Maybe, just maybe, he'd get one of them today.

'You. Let. Them. *Marry.*'

Louve's eyes widened and his expression darkened. 'It's been six years since you've been home. Three years since you've known. One friend is dead, the other is pregnant, and *this* is what you want to talk about?'

Bury your past... Maybe not everything, but he *would* have answers as to why Louve hadn't warned him. 'Yes.'

Louve wrapped the reins around his wrists. 'You left and didn't return—made no mention of returning either. What game do you play with this false blame?'

'This is my home.'

'This is a property you've despised all your life. You barely touched the fields after your father's death. You hate the very soil you're now stepping on. You *left*.'

'You knew how I felt about her.' Nicholas shut down the memories of them racing horses, her pealing laughter, her daring him to catch her. Every tenant, all their neighbours, even France must have heard their unfettered joy. The certainty of a match between them. 'It was hardly a secret.'

'Even so...' Louve unwound the reins and shook them. 'Your letters to her stopped.'

'And you didn't enquire?'

'You didn't mention it either.'

'You want me to tell you *now*? Is that why you dragged me out here? It can't have been to till this useless field.'

Louve's oxen jumped forward, dragging him along until he wrenched them under control again. 'You can't be blaming me when *you* should have mentioned something. Anything. You were my friend. *They* were my friends. Trying to keep the peace was more difficult than your battles.'

'Clearly.' Nicholas pointed to his eye patch and

was glad when Louve didn't glance away. 'Tell me what you haven't told me.'

'Only if you tell me why you want to know. You've returned, and yet you act like you don't want to be here.'

'I don't. Just the same, I want to know.'

Louve tilted his head, considering his words.

Nicholas didn't intend to say any more. He'd said enough.

Louve exhaled roughly. '*Dammit.* As children, we were *all* half in love with her—until she only wanted you. But for Roger and me those feelings didn't just go away. We were both still a little in love with her.'

'I was *absolutely* in love with her!' Nicholas growled.

'You stopped writing to her. She was our friend, more like our sister than any family we had. She…was broken. Roger and I picked up the pieces you left behind.'

Louve was lying. The Matilda Nicholas had left would never have broken. She'd defied him up to the end. A couple of missing letters wouldn't have made her change her heart.

He pictured the scenario of Louve and Roger, swooping on her like vultures. 'I can imagine those pieces.'

Louve's expression turned fierce. 'We did not touch her. Nothing until it was almost too late. If you don't like the consequences, then you should have replied.'

His sweat was chilling the clothes on his body, but nothing felt as cold as Louve's words.

'Replied?'

'You might have stopped your correspondence, but they didn't stop theirs. I didn't write, but Roger and Matilda...'

'I received that letter,' he bit out. So much agony when he'd lost his eye, but that letter had been worse. He didn't want to remember that letter.

'Then why didn't you reply?'

Because he hadn't been able to. Because a sword had sliced across his heart and stolen his eye. By the time he'd been physically able to reply it had been far too late.

Snapping his reins, he forced the oxen to move again. Forced himself to continue. He heard

Louve shout, but he ignored it. Another turn and the whole field would be done. This time he welcomed his bleeding hands. The pain was nothing to what he felt inside him.

It had been too late to reply to Matilda's letter. The letter that had told him she was to be married. But to this day he loved to torture himself with 'what ifs'. What if he'd received her letter *before* they'd married and been able to stop it?

He knew the answer to that, too. He couldn't have stopped it. He had purposely not written to them because he hadn't want to notify his enemies that he cared for others. He couldn't have protected them.

In truth, it had been too late for all of them the moment he'd become a hired sword. If only...

Still, he had expected his friends to remain honourable, not to desire his betrothed. Which showed how young and naïve he'd truly been.

He glanced over his shoulder at Louve, driving his oxen just as fiercely as he. He, too, was stronger than he had been in their youth, and there was still something honourable in him.

The estate had prospered under his care. Why wouldn't Matilda want him, or he her?

Another turn was all Louve allowed him. It was all he allowed himself.

Louve threw the reins to one side and stormed around his oxen to face Nicholas. 'No more running. No more distractions. The damn field can wait.'

'*You* brought me out here.'

'To deal with Roger's death. I didn't know of the rest!'

'That I thought you had betrayed me as well? What else was I to think? They *married*. If they could do that then—'

'Then I had allowed it? I didn't simply *allow* them to marry. You think I didn't talk to Roger? To Matilda? You think I could have stopped them?'

'If not for me, maybe yourself, since you're in love with her as well!'

'You're jealous! My God. You love her still. But if you feel this way now, you must have felt it then.'

'Would it have changed anything?' Nicholas

asked, even though he didn't want the answer. He didn't. Because either way it would be like the sword through his eye again, and this time it would take his heart.

Louve's expression darkened with determination. 'Why didn't you write to her? Do you know what she faced from the tenants and neighbours when your letters stopped? And it was made all the worse when you wrote to me and not her. *Why?* Her mother had died. Her father was unstable. She had to bear all of that alone.'

He'd borne his burdens alone as well, but instead of resentment at Louve's words, he felt Matilda's pain against his already open wound. Her mother had died. Had he known? Had he been told? If so, it had not been by Matilda, and that gutted him. He hadn't been fit to be with her, and yet he'd done it because of her.

'I couldn't write to her,' he said.

Shock and then understanding flashed on Louve's face. 'You and your coin. What danger did you court for it to cost you this much?'

More danger than he wanted to talk about today—and it wasn't over.

'You need to talk to her. She needs to know.'

'She married him and is pregnant with his child. She made her choice, and it's as final as the grave.'

'Roger's...gone.' Louve swallowed hard. 'If you—'

'He's gone, but his decision—*her* decision—is not. What is done is done.'

Nothing was resolved. More lies...more betrayal. Rather than have this conversation he'd face Reynold of the Warstone family again, or the bastard who'd taken his eye. He certainly didn't want to face *himself*. He'd had adversity since he'd left Mei Solis, but he'd come to terms with it. He'd had a life, and it had been a good one. Or so he'd thought.

But Mei Solis had been a dagger in his side. And when she'd married Roger, Matilda had shoved that dagger deeper and he'd been bleeding ever since.

He'd received just one lone letter, and her actions had spoken of where her heart was. He'd thought he had given them his blessing long ago. Let them have their marriage and Mei Solis. And yet when he'd seen Rhain's happiness he had known something festered in him. Something that wouldn't give him peace.

But now, since returning here, he didn't even recognise himself or his actions.

A noise across the field captured his gaze. Boys were racing towards them, the dimming light making them barely discernible. How many hours had they been out here?

Louve exhaled roughly. 'They're here to take the oxen and the ploughs in. We need more time.'

Nicholas considered the man before him. All these years he'd imagined the plots the three of them had made, but perhaps Louve had been a bystander to it all. Truly, what could Louve have done if Roger had wanted Matilda and she him?

'You truly talked to them, didn't you?'

Louve rubbed his jaw, pointed at Nicholas. 'I talked to them both together, and even to Bess. To Rohesia, to her father. I suggest you do the same.'

'No.'

'But—

'No!' He put as much emphasis on the word

as he had effort in tilling the field. Talking hadn't worked in the past and it wouldn't now. His anger was still against a dead man and a pregnant woman. His sense of betrayal against Louve, however, was gone.

'Well, then… I could use some ale,' Louve said, raising his hands. Blood poured from them.

Nicholas loosened his hold on the reins. They were numb, bloodied, and as broken as the rest of him. 'Do you have any mead?'

Louve grinned. 'From a neighbour who owed us much. A whole barrel full.'

Maybe it was the words finally shared, his friend's attempt at humour, or the fact that he would get blinding drunk tonight, but Nicholas's heart eased just a little. 'You take the ale. The mead is mine…*after* we bandage our hands.'

'You need your wounds licked? I knew you'd gone soft, Mercenary.'

'Not soft, but practical. I need to hold two flagons of mead, and these useless appendages won't do it on their own.'

Chapter Six

Another feast was laid out, since Cook had been able to salvage most of the finest cuts and dishes from the night before. Not that it mattered, since the Lord of Mei Solis hadn't arrived to appreciate her effort.

There were more in attendance than the night before. Most likely come to see what other events might take place today. The weather was certainly foreshadowing something portentous, with the temperature dropping and a darkening sky, and the fact that two very capable men seemed to have disappeared.

'Are you certain the teams are out of the wind?' Matilda hugged herself and rubbed her hands against her arms. Despite the repairs, a bitter wind still seeped into the manor.

Bess shrugged. 'The boys went out when it was turning dark and helped the men bring the teams and ploughs in to be protected.'

But Nicholas and Louve had walked off and hadn't been seen since. She still couldn't believe Nicholas and Louve had ploughed the fallow fields. *She* was the one who'd stood in the graveyard trying to talk sense into Nicholas. Louve's strategy had been to waste a day of hard labour. The fact that they were now gone meant it had either worked, and they were bonding, or one of them was dead and the other had run off.

Either way, she didn't understand it. 'How did this come about?'

Bess gave her a pointed look. 'You don't understand why Nicholas took a swing at Louve or their male bravado?'

'Both.'

Bess laughed, then looked more closely at Matilda's face. She shrugged. 'Oh! You're being truthful. Both happened because of *you*.'

'Me?' *Ridiculous.* Maybe Louve had felt obliged to say something in her honour, but Nicholas wouldn't care what was said. 'If that's true—which it can't be—what would be the purpose?'

She could imagine Nicholas's umbrage if she had married Roger behind Nicholas's back. But that wasn't what had happened. Nicholas had stopped writing to her, and in doing so had broken their betrothal.

'I told you to wait,' Bess said, lowering her voice. 'That with your mother's death and your father's demands it wasn't—'

'Not this.' Matilda interrupted her. 'Not now.'

'If not now, when?' Bess looked away, blinking rapidly. 'I know with Roger—'

'I *loved* him.'

Bess laid her hand over Matilda's. 'I know you did, but there was always concern over when Nicholas returned.'

'There was no concern at all.' None of them had seen the look in Nicholas's eyes when he'd left. After she had pleaded with her heart, with words and tears… If he'd been able to leave her then, there was no reason for his return now.

Yet the past and its possibilities haunted her still. Back then with every heartbeat she had waited, and her heart had broken. Then her mother had died. There had been barely anything left of her when Roger had proposed. She'd told him so, and he'd still wanted her. Wanted to protect and defend her.

And now Roger, who had always been stalwart and dependable, was dead. Matilda still couldn't grasp it. If not for the pricking grief in her chest from tears she refused to shed, she'd believe him no farther away than in his beloved fields.

It had always been he who shielded her, who had defended Louve and Nicholas. Even when Louve had questioned their marrying; when Nicholas hadn't replied to Roger's letter…or hers.

She didn't deserve his unwavering loyalty and neither did they. Where could they be? It was dangerous to be out on a night such as this.

'To plough that field is useless. What kind of behaviour is this?'

Bess patted her hand, where it still clutched her arm. 'Your three closest friends were boys. I'm surprised you don't know that this is absolutely male behaviour.'

'But Roger and Louve never behaved that way together, so—'

The bellow of an unsteady song heralded Nicholas and Louve's grand entrance, and the Great Doors bursting open ensured that everyone turned to witness the great event of their inebriation.

'See there! They're hale and well!' Bess said, her lips tight with holding back laughter. 'Nothing to be worried about at all.'

Matilda wasn't worried—she was furious. Anticipating something important after their time in the graveyard together, she was shocked at this irreverent arrival.

Louve was singing off-key; Nicholas was waving his arm to keep the uneven beat. Arms around each other's shoulders, they entered the hall sideways, which made their floundering balance look not unlike reeds being felled by the scythe.

Louve's hair was parted on the wrong side, while Nicholas's fell long without his *queue*. Their clothes were rumpled, muddy from the field, and blades of grass stuck to their shoes. But the wetness of their fronts, their hair, and along the side of their legs, as if they'd been splashed with water, was…

They were taking stumbling steps closer, disentangled now, and Louve was adjusting his tunic, Nicholas straightening to his full height. Both were undeniably proud as they greeted the tenants with smiles and laughter on the way to her and Bess.

Closer yet, and Matilda had no words. For it wasn't water that soaked their clothing.

They smelled, even from a distance, of sweet mead. Which only made her more cross. *Mead.* Flagons full, if they'd wasted that much. It was a commodity she knew nothing about—hidden somewhere on the land so that she couldn't serve it nor have some for herself.

Mead wasn't made on Mei Solis, so Louve must have bargained something, which he'd thought to hide from her. Except now he'd shared it with Nicholas.

'Mind if I stay here?' Bess asked.

'Would you move if I told you to?' Matilda said.

'Not a chance!' Bess chuckled.

'Such frowns, Matilda,' said Louve. 'Look who I brought in from the fields!'

Matilda eyed Nicholas. With his hair loose, a tendril hanging over his eye patch, he looked... *dishevelled.* Thoughts unbidden came as she noticed the wave of his hair against his masculine jaw, and how the mead had softened his lips and his gaze.

He looked for all the world as if he'd just got out of bed. And the fact that she noticed such details startled her. She shouldn't be noticing any such details about Nicholas.

She kept her eyes on Louve, who was with certainty more inebriated than Nicholas. If someone had brought someone else in, it was most likely Nicholas who had brought Louve to the hall.

'It doesn't look like you came from the fields but from the ale stores,' she said. 'Except it's not ale I smell. Where did you get the mead?'

'And did you get any of it in your mouths?' Bess asked.

Her tone sounded appalled, but her eyes were too lively. Her friend wanted to laugh, and was only holding it back because of her.

Louve wagged a finger at Matilda and frowned at Bess's response. In full concentration, ready for a retort, he looked as if he was ten years of age again.

'The barrel was…uncooperative in releasing its contents.' Nicholas shook his sleeve, as if that would release the dampness there.

'Over both of you?' Bess quipped. 'It looks like you played in it.'

'You fought with a barrel of mead?' Matilda loved mead—which was beside the point now, but counted in the long list of offences they had committed.

'I believe the mead's now winning.' Louve shifted unevenly.

'Come, let us retire,' Nicholas said.

'Retire?' Matilda said.

'I couldn't sit through a meal,' Louve replied.

'Maybe you should have thought of that earlier.'

'Oh, I stopped *thinking* long ago,' Louve said.

Matilda felt Nicholas watching her. She knew she was terse, and probably sounded snappish as well. Normally she wouldn't care if Louve got drunk, but this was Nicholas's return feast, second time around, and she was depending on it running smoothly. That meant they must all dine around the table together.

'Then it's all well and good that it is tomorrow morning we shall be discussing the estate,' Nicholas said.

'Morning?' Louve muttered. 'Vengeful bastard...'

'After that last goblet of yours "slipped", absolutely in the morning.' Nicholas gestured. 'I'll take you up.'

'You *can't.*' Matilda couldn't believe that Nicholas was entertaining the idea of not dining with everyone. She wouldn't allow it.

At her words, Nicholas turned. Other than his appearance, nothing in his mien gave any indication of intoxication or weakness. His gaze was steady, his bearing proud. 'Since I'll be retiring as well, it seems most expedient.'

A mercenary's stare wouldn't frighten her. 'You weren't here last night. Cook has saved your favourite dishes, and there are tenants in attendance who wish to celebrate your return.'

Nicholas tilted his head, as if he was studying her. 'Let them celebrate, then.'

'I'll take him up,' Bess said.

'I can take myself,' Louve interjected. 'My legs feel suddenly very steady.'

Bess snorted, and Matilda watched her two friends make a hasty retreat.

There was only one gaze on her now. Nicholas was still watching her. So she schooled her features to look as serene as she hoped she'd actually be some day.

Nicholas was definitely not as drunk as Louve, and nor was he in as jovial a mood as he'd been when he'd entered. Had she *ever* seen him play around like that? Of course she had—before he'd left. They all had. It was just that even in a mere day of his returning she somehow knew he hadn't played like that in a long time.

And, though he might have stopped keeping time to Louve's terrible song the moment the Great Doors had banged open, there had still been something resembling happiness as he'd looped his way into the hall and greeted a few of his tenants.

It had done something to his warrior's features. Giving her glimpses of the man he'd used to be and also of the man he now was. Indomitable. Fierce. A mercenary, but still devastatingly handsome. After everything, how could he be attractive?

Whatever serenity she had tried to achieve slipped away, and she let it. If composure allowed her to realise that Nicholas was as striking as he'd ever been, she didn't need it. She needed defences, barriers, and her ire again.

Especially since Nicholas stood in front of her now and there wasn't a trace of the friendship he had shown with Louve, and he no longer looked freshly woken from an evening sharing someone's bed. Now he was all cold formality and something else that scraped along her skin. Like a warning.

When the corners of Nicholas's lips curved into a pitiless smile, she knew that a mercenary's stare might not scare her, but she did wonder whether a mercenary would kill her.

'It seems you've got your wish to keep me here, Matilda,' Nicholas said. 'Now, what do you intend to do with me?'

Nicholas relished Matilda's wary eyes and jutted chin. Surprisingly, not because he knew his words had made her uneasy—though there was an aspect of that—but because in this moment she was all contradictions. Demanding he stay for the meal, and yet cautious, because he, too, was unpredictable.

In this moment, Matilda was completely un-predictable...but familiar. This was the Matilda he recognised. The composed woman who'd greeted him upon his arrival he didn't know and didn't care for. She didn't fit. Not that anything between them *fitted*.

'Since I am to stay down in this hall, I expect to be fed well.'

Her eyes narrowed. 'You would have been fed better last night.'

He didn't hide his smirk. She didn't like his imperious demands? *Fine*. He didn't like being here. 'It seems the drink has whetted my appetite.'

She glanced to the stairs. 'How much did he drink?'

'We matched goblet for goblet.'

Too much, and not enough. He had always been able to hold his ale more than the next man.

Today he'd wanted to get blind drunk, but he had no desire to carry Louve at the end of it.

With sweet mead and thwarted revenge running through his veins, the fact that he hadn't been able to get passing-out-drunk galled him. Since Matilda wanted to keep him here, he'd make sure she felt some of his bitterness.

He was desperate to forget his need for apologies and revenge. Yet here he was, not drunk and not sober, and certainly all too aware that he could not start demanding retribution from a woman who was currently rubbing her swollen belly.

'Louve rarely drinks,' she said. 'He'll be ill without food.'

Her loyalty to Louve was freshly added to his tally of irritations, though he couldn't understand why. 'Bess will know what to do—and I require food as well.'

Her eyes were lowered and raised. Fleetingly, but he felt as if she was *noticing* him. Yet when her eyes met his again there was no seduction there. Was she aware of what she'd done? Or maybe she'd done nothing at all. It was most likely the drink that had him imagining Matilda had noticed him.

'I'm certain you can take care of yourself,' she said.

And even though her voice was sharper than before, and her eyes held some frustration that appeared different from her irritation earlier, he couldn't shake the tightening of his body at her words. How much mead had he drunk?

He couldn't—shouldn't—feel this way for this woman, and yet even her words were suggestive. It was too long since he'd imbibed…even longer since he'd had a woman.

She'd insisted on holding him here for her sense of celebration. As if he owed anything to the tenants here. He'd cared for them well while he'd been absent. His presence here actually impaired them, since he was not out earning more coin.

He didn't need to be here. He needed to be upstairs, with food and a bath brought.

He felt almost feral in all his denied desires. And. Yet. She. Kept. Him. Here.

'I intended to take care of myself,' he said, 'but how could I have denied your kind request?'

Her eyes narrowed. 'I didn't *request* you to dine. This is your home and you should *want* to eat here.'

He gestured to the remaining seats. 'Never truer words were said. I *would* like to eat here—thank you, Matilda.'

With a scathing look, Matilda strode towards the waiting chairs, ensuring that he followed her. It was as if she was the one who dictated when they ate or who had the most power here.

They sat, and it was as if the crowd drew a collective sigh. Servants immediately brought trenchers and dishes. Matilda sat stiffly next to him, allowing him to choose the different courses to spread on their shared trencher.

He saw that everyone else was already seated and eating. Consequently the food selection was disappearing before his eyes. Feeling the mead in his veins, he piled what food he could onto the trencher.

'I see you do not keep custom with the tenants

waiting until the Lord of the Manor is seated before they sit and begin eating.'

His father had always insisted that tenants or guests weren't to sit until the Lord sat. It was a common courtesy, but one he'd found overbearing given that the manor was a simple one.

'It made no sense. You left three of us in charge.'

He had left three friends in charge and returned to find only one.

Trying to distract himself from his darker thoughts, he spoke with others, tore into his lamb. He watched Matilda become quiet and pick at her food.

She was uncomfortable dining with him. *Good.* Since she had demanded he stay, she should have to live with the consequences.

Matilda couldn't get anything past the restriction in her throat. There was nothing to be done, regardless of the words she and Nicholas had exchanged. *Nothing.*

She had ordered specialities to be baked and certain dishes to be cooked in celebration of Nicholas's return. She might not want it, but he was the Lord of Mei Solis. This was his home, and others would look at this night as a cause for celebration.

But she was all too aware of Nicholas—of how his eyes darted from his food to his drink to those around him. And to her. She felt him watching *her.*

Maybe it was her resentment that fuelled her awareness of him. Or perhaps it was his injury.

His injury was most prominent. The dark slash of leather over his eye worn like a tunic or a pair of breeches. Soft-looking, like a favourite pair of boots. But something about the way he moved his head, or the sudden brush of his hand at his nape, made her think perhaps the patch *wasn't* worn as easily as his boots.

And then there was his scar—thin, well-healed. Jagged from the forced slicing of his skin, from the rugged contours of his face. It should have diminished his presence somehow. The loss of his eye should have made him less of a man. But it didn't. It made him different, darker. Intimidating. And it didn't mar his natural beauty.

But then Nicholas had always held some command that went beyond his position at Mei Solis. He still held some fascination that she had thought long-lost. Especially after he'd broken their betrothal and her heart. And yet, for her, he was still rivetingly handsome.

Maybe even more so.

The leather strip covered some of his scar, but there was something...*wicked* about the way it looked. She shouldn't notice that. Certainly not when she was pregnant...not when she'd married another.

Roger.

There came a piercing of grief in her chest that she fought against. She hadn't dared let herself grieve for her husband. She'd shed tears while she had tried saving him, and they'd done her no good. She couldn't—wouldn't—shed them now, when they were useless. *Useless.*

Perhaps some time in Nicholas's company would destroy whatever misguided feeling still lingered. If she could wrest it from her heart and destroy it, all the better. He didn't deserve any feelings from her at all.

He didn't deserve her to be watching him as he conversed with his tenants. As he ate the food placed before him as if it pleased him. As he idly scanned the hall, taking in all the changes.

At one time she would have cared what he thought of the hall and the furnishings she'd had made for it. She would have asked about the food, all of it finer than when he had left. She'd spent years of her life ensuring that when he returned he would have the home they had wanted. She had been able to do so because Nicholas had sent more silver than she'd ever thought possible. Silver that she, Roger and Louve had carefully divided.

Then had come the realisation that Nicholas might never return—or at least never to her. So the coin allocated to home decoration had been given to the tenants. Only Cook had received the original budget, to make improvements on the food, because that was shared with everyone.

It was sumptuous fare tonight, with candied nuts and fruit, and extra honey on the fritters. Cook had indeed provided treats in honour of the Lord of the Manor's return.

All the food smelled delicious, and she was starving. Yet every time she glanced at their trencher to carve some meat, or reached for her goblet, she watched Nicholas reach for his.

Why had she insisted on him attending this feast?

Nicholas had ignored Matilda through a few of the courses, and was finding the evening as long as he had thought it would be. Worse, he had garnered more than a few questioning glances from his tenants. He knew he was being rude, but he was loath to converse with Matilda when he'd drunk so much, was exhausted from the fields, and burned with the need for a revenge that would never happen.

More, he was loath to talk with Matilda when their only conversation so far had been filled with animosity. Sharp jabs at each other in the graveyard.

Yet as the meal wore on, and the mead wore off, he knew that sitting there with such a strain between them wouldn't solve anything. Burying the past wouldn't happen unless he could find some common ground. Even if only for this evening. But what?

He took a sip of the watered ale that tasted bitter after the fine mead. Why hadn't he requested a few more flagons to share with everyone for this meal?

'Is the ale not to your liking?' Matilda asked.

Was he so transparent? He'd felt selfish when he had remembered that she liked mead, and now had to drink the same bitter ale that he did. However, did she ask him because she was a 'friend', for want of a better word, or because she was Bailiff and had control over such matters?

So much confusion between them… But that didn't mean he couldn't be cordial. 'It's well enough. The food, however, is very fine.'

He knew he'd said the correct thing when a little of her stiffness lessened. 'Cook has more help, and for the most part she and I organise the meals while someone else actually prepares them.'

'I'd forgotten how many of our meals went wrong,' he said, and couldn't help but smile. 'Like the Great Goose Fat Debacle.'

'How could you forget?' she said. 'Poor Bernice didn't have eyebrows for a year.'

'Which fact you didn't let her forget for several years afterwards. You were relentless in teasing her. The things you would do and say!'

Matilda tore at some bread, but she didn't raise it to her lips and she kept her gaze downward-facing.

He watched her as she continued to face away from him, a frown between her brows. She was suddenly quiet. Had he hurt her? Why would he care? He'd travelled many weeks in order to arrive here and hurt her, and now, with one turn of her head, he found himself with another goal. To make her look at him again.

It had always been the depth of her hazel eyes that took his breath—as if life shimmered there in all its glory, and he only had to stare long enough to understand it. For a moment, while they'd talked of Bernice, he'd thought he saw something familiar in them, but now the light was dim, as if she was purposely trying to dampen her spirit.

She glanced up at him. Briefly.

Though he didn't understand it, he had clearly hurt her with that remark. Did she not *want* to remember past mischiefs when they were mere children? Those, despite all else, were still sweet memories for him. It was only after they'd grown up that matters had turned bitter.

He tried again. 'The hall's had changes...'

Matilda parted her lips as if she wanted to say something, then shook her head. It was as if she didn't want to talk of the hall and all she had done here.

No matter. He could accept that she'd done well. There was comforts instead of austerity. Repair instead of debris. Numerous thick dark tables and benches filled the once empty space, and padded chairs graced both ends. His father had always held two high-backed chairs at one end. Now there were places for four people to be held in honour, and he didn't need to guess who those four would have been.

Before his thoughts turned dark again, he said, 'You made these changes a while ago?'

She shrugged.

He appreciated the extra sconces, and the

heavy linens that surrounded the large entrance doors, but one change intrigued him. His father had repaired the hearth so that it functioned, but there was new masonry surrounding it, carved with horses. The horses were riderless, wild, and within the fire's flames and shadows they seemed to soar across the masonry.

'Your carvings are beautiful,' he said.

'My what?'

'The horses on the mantel—they look as if they are riding free.'

Her eyes were wide. 'How did you know I carved them?'

'Who else reveres horses as much as you?'

She turned towards him. 'I neither carved nor drew when you were last here.'

'But you wanted to.'

'You remember that?'

It was his turn to shrug.

She looked over his shoulder. 'I did carve them, and I thank you for your compliment, but I no longer ride.'

'I suppose not, with your pregnancy...'

'Before then.'

Maybe it was the mead, still affecting him, but he thought he could not be hearing correctly. 'I refuse to believe that.'

'It wasn't sensible.'

'That was what Roger used to say,' he scoffed. 'You used to tease him about it.'

'Maybe I saw the error of my ways.'

He shook his head. Now he *knew* he was hearing things wrongly. 'Galloping across open fields so you could feel the whip of the wind against your face? That was an *error*? If so, you have surely depicted the joy of it with great care and skill on *my* fireplace.'

She gasped and turned pale.

Then the truth hit him. 'You didn't voluntarily stop riding. Roger *made* you.'

'That's not true.'

She was too quick in her denial, and he knew that she knew it when she grabbed her goblet and took a drink to hide her expression.

He wanted to laugh, but the laugh lodged in his throat. Denying Matilda the joy of riding would have been the perfect revenge. However, Roger or someone else had beaten him to it.

'If Roger didn't make you do it, then who stopped you? Because horses were your *life*. Jumping and clearing those hedges—that was the Matilda who seized life.'

Matilda stood, her chair scraping loudly across the floor. Those few still dining turned their heads to watch them. 'That Matilda is no more. Pardon me, Nicholas. I am suddenly very tired from…my day.'

He wanted to argue, but now their conversation was no longer private. Instead, he popped some dried fruit in his mouth and watched her walk through the Great Doors. When they had closed behind her Nicholas waved his arm and requested a flagon of un-watered stout.

He'd probably be sick before morning, but he didn't care. He wanted to get blind drunk, and in that he would succeed.

But he'd count it his only successes this evening. Travelling here, he'd wanted to hurt Matilda, and tonight he had—several times. Only he didn't know why or how. He did know, however, that something inside him didn't like it.

It was useless to take his revenge against a

dead man and a pregnant woman. No matter how wronged he felt, something he hadn't even been aware of rebelled against hurting Matilda.

When she'd stood up, there had been tears in her eyes before she'd bade him goodnight, told him how she was tired of him. She'd tried to cover up her words, but he'd heard what she'd truly wanted to say. And he knew it was the truth. Because she'd told him she was tired of him once before.

Matilda always had been able to slay him with words. It was what had felled him that first time. Not the sword gutting his eye, but Matilda's words on a parchment, received while he lay on a pallet in Spain.

His injuries had been raw open wounds then, and Rhain had sat diligently by his side. No one had thought he'd live—not even himself. Then, on that fateful rainy day when Rhain had returned to the room, Nicholas had known something was different because of the quickness of Rhain's feet across the floorboards, when normally he trod carefully. Different, too, because of the smile on Rhain's face as he'd sat down on a stool and showed him the correspondence.

In those early days he had hardly known his name through the pain racking his body. The feeling that knives still slashed his face. The agonising *loss*.

Yet even so he had recognised that Rhain held a missive from Mei Solis. From Matilda.

In that realisation there had been no agony. There had been joy. He'd stopped writing to her months before, to protect her from his enemies. Soon after she'd ceased writing to him. To receive a missive when he hadn't expected one had given him hope when he'd had none.

He'd been fighting his pain, fighting not to die. But after a month of fever and the loss of blood, of foul poultices and prodding, and days when he hadn't slept and weeks when he'd done nothing, he'd been losing the strength to continue. In those days he'd thought Matilda would be better without him. No woman would want a man as disfigured as he.

But when Rhain had sat next to him and showed him that slip of parchment it had been like seeing reinforcements hurtling over the hill in a battle he was losing. If he could have smiled he would have. He knew that tears had pricked his eyes while new strength had coursed through him.

And then had come that shadow over his friend's expression as he'd opened the correspondence and viewed its contents. Slight, but enough. A shot of alarm had passed through him and he had demanded that Rhain read it. When Rhain had kept silent he'd struggled to rise from the pallet, to fight with Rhain, who had barked about his stitches as he'd held him down.

He hadn't cared about himself because he'd been certain that something had happened to Matilda.

Rhain had known that, and had choked out the words.

Matilda had married Roger and wrote to tell him she would never write to him again.

Nicholas pushed his chair away from the table and surveyed the now empty hall. He'd stayed to the end of the meal and ensured that a defence-less woman carrying a child understood his hatred. He couldn't even take pleasure in knowing that he'd tried to warn her. That if she'd only let him rest in his own chamber none of this would have occurred.

He took no satisfaction in the fact that he'd been right. For once he wished this long battle he waged with his past would cease.

But it wouldn't happen tonight.

And most likely not tomorrow either.

Slowly, he walked up the stairs, finally to sleep, to rest, grateful that there were no servants blocking his way. He would obtain at least one relief tonight. In sleep, he'd have a few hours of reprieve from his memories. When he woke, it would all start again.

There had been a time when Nicholas would have offered both his eyes to keep Matilda. But with that one letter, with those few words from Matilda in her uneven handwriting, Nicholas had known that no sword could ever cut him deeper.

Chapter Seven

Early morning, and Nicholas's head hurt like hell. But he'd asked for a meeting with Louve and Matilda, and it would be done.

No vengeance—and no fields to plough today. His body, and his hands reminded him sharply that training to kill another man wasn't the same as farming the land.

Farming. He owned this land, and it was his inheritance, but he'd fought against it all his life. Still, there were duties here, and conferring with his steward and his bailiff was one of them.

Although exactly what he would discuss at this meeting, he didn't know.

When people saw him for the first time it was always the same. Some looked him straight in the eye, but he could see the tightness in their expressions as they attempted to be friendly. Some found the task more difficult, and gave open grimaces when they got close enough to see the scar on his neck. Always, *always*, they imagined it happening to them.

He always wanted to tell them that it hadn't hurt. Not at first—not in the moment when it had happened. There had been only a void. A ringing in his ears as his body caved underneath the injury. He had felt the hard ground more than the sting of the gash.

That sting had come later, when they'd moved him. But not when he been lying on the ground. Then his body had thought him dead; he'd thought himself dead. No strength in his arms or his legs. His body hadn't brought up the rush of pain until they'd put him on a pallet and rushed him off the battlefield.

And *then* that pain… He winced even to remember it.

There were times he felt it still, on the periphery of his memory. Pricking at him when he worked too hard. When he gave a certain swing to his sword that was similar to the one he had made that day it would flash back in his memory. Like a ghost that kept brushing against him.

In strangers, he expected and was used to this reactions. But, surprisingly, he somehow thought he wouldn't receive those looks of pity or horror here in his home.

When Matilda had been betrothed to him, he had imagined her by his side—imagined their shared looks as they ate. Imagined how close they'd sit, the intimate touches of their fingers and hands above and below the table.

He was tired, but this—this meeting he wanted done or he'd never rest. His council had once been his close friends.

When he'd left he had believed such a meeting would be full of ale and talk. Full of smiles and relief. He would have returned with coin enough for Helena, and for Mei Solis. Enough silver to give everything he'd ever wanted to Matilda. He'd imagined Roger and Louve to have been betrothed, if not found wives. He'd imagined returning happy. Whole.

Instead, he was missing one eye and most of his heart.

'Ah, here you are.' Louve strode down the stairs and into the room adjacent to the hall. Smaller, more confined, it had a fireplace and a few chairs. A place to go on a chilly day in a draughty manor. 'Is she not here yet?' he asked.

'You're early.'

'I didn't mean to be. The sheer amount of times I had to piss in the night kept me awake. You didn't have that problem, or I would've stumbled past you in the passageway. Why are *you* up early?'

Nicholas shrugged. He hadn't been able to stay in his room and hadn't been able to bear the conversations that would take place if he sat in the hall.

Louve collapsed in a chair. 'Could we do this without talking numbers?'

'Did you keep ledgers?'

'Matilda insisted.'

'I'll look at them later.'

Louve slumped even more in his chair. 'Since Matilda isn't here, should we head down to the cellar?'

The cellar...where they kept the few weapons

they had, and where iron bars protected their silver. There had never been any coin chests there except once, when Helena had arrived. At that time his father had built the bars and the shelves. Then he had carefully put the chests in the room, with the few swords and shields, locked them, and held the keys himself.

His father had expected that silver to grow, but coin by coin it had disappeared.

The cellar was dark—not only with lack of light, but with past disappointment. It was the last place he wanted to visit at Mei Solis. Though soon he'd need to. If only to give Louve credit for taking care of the manor.

'You want to start there because there is no light to hurt your head?' asked Nicholas.

'Too true—but this meeting is official, is it not? We are to discuss what we have done for Mei Solis while you show us what is in those satchels.'

'My satchels? They're in the bedroom. Still full of coin.'

Louve's brow arched. 'Three satchels' worth of coin and nothing to protect them?'

Three satchels' worth and far more coin than Helena had brought with her that day.

'You haven't been here for six years,' Louve said.

'Do you foresee a problem with that?'

'No, but I find it fascinating.'

'That I brought silver? Or that I think a bedroom is as secure as that dungeon my father created?'

'That you now seem to trust. It wasn't your strongest suit when we were children.'

He had his father and all his broken promises to thank for that.

'How could I trust either you *or* Roger? The moment I let my guard down thistles were stuck in my braies or a bucket of piss was poured over my head.'

'That bucket missed you.'

'Not for lack of trying.'

'True… I told Roger we should have had a back-up pail, so that when you stepped aside the other would dunk you, but you know what he was like…'

Pulling pranks but defending those he played them on. He shut those thoughts down.

'You gave as good as you got…better,' Louve continued.

Nicholas knew where this conversation was going. 'You deserved that.'

'To this day, I can't believe I didn't smell it.'

'I made certain you couldn't. You'd had a flagon of ale. A herd of horses wouldn't have woken you.'

'But the dung was spread all around my bed…'

Nicholas laughed. It was a good memory. 'Not my idea! I only wanted to get you drunk and stick your hand in some water so you'd piss yourself. You stepped in it.'

'Slipped on my backside in it!' Louve said in mock anger.

'As if you didn't think it was funny!'

'Only after I'd had my retribution.' Louve shook his head. 'That made up for the trouble we were in afterwards. That was what Matilda said, didn't she? She was the devil, she was. Could talk us into anything.'

She had. With a dancing light in her eyes to

let them know she wasn't serious, but words as firm as any judgement day. Those three boys had followed whatever antics she'd thought up. Because they'd had the stupidity and the brawn to really cause havoc, and she'd had all the mischief. And the ideas...

Matilda... Already he saw she had changed. Or maybe he was imagining it. He'd thought he saw traces of the old Matilda last night at dinner. There had been moments when he'd thought she'd chuck a turnip at him.

But maybe she'd truly changed. Louve had said 'was', as if her mischief was in the past.

He inwardly shook himself. He'd been gone too long, and who she was now wasn't his concern. Remembering how she was, reminiscing, would do him no good.

It had been bad enough when he had been expected to reside in a room that haunted him. He didn't need the rest of the rooms in Mei Solis taunting him.

In his father's old room a full, deeply carved four-poster took up most of the space. A table and two padded chairs were placed by the windows for intimate dining or conversation. There was a thick, elaborate bench by the fireplace.

Large enough for two.

Large enough to hold a family.

There was even a small table next to it, on which to place a flagon of warmed mead or ale.

The whole room was masculine except for the fabric decorations, some patterned with flowers in red and green. They weren't necessary, but lavish. Just as he'd told Matilda to make it.

He hadn't expected the more significant details of the room. The fact that the table, the chairs, the bed...all of it...were made for his size. For *him*. She would have told the carpenters that. Thought of that detail. Because he certainly hadn't.

Why would he? Most of his life he'd never fitted inside huts, inns, lodgings or even fine castles. If there was a bed, he simply pulled the mattress off the frame and laid it on the floor. Mostly he'd order extra blankets, so they'd fit from his shoulders to cover his feet.

But this room had been made with care...with love. She had made a room for *him*—for *them*—

with the idea that he would be master of Mei Solis and she its mistress.

Why had he returned? He could argue that this was his home, and that he had every right to inhabit it. But Mei Solis had never been his home, and he had been all too eager to leave it. He could argue that now he had no duties with Rhain and the other mercenaries, no requests from King Edward, he had nowhere else to go.

Which wasn't true either.

'Why are we in here?' Matilda asked.

'Because it is quiet—or it *was*,' Louve quipped.

Her eyes were wary, but the rest of her was as bright as sunshine on snow. Her cheeks were red, her wavy hair was plaited back and seemed crisp. Her large cloak, silk-lined, hid her belly, but even so she held some inner light, and he turned his gaze away before she caught him staring.

Six years away…three years knowing she'd chosen another. He was a mercenary, a knight, and yet in these glances he felt like a fumbling lovesick fool.

It was temporary, he told himself again. He'd

returned because Rhain had said he must bury his past. And he would do so by spending more time with Matilda and Louve. Would free himself of whatever this was inside him. Some remnant of friendship. Of love. Ghost feelings that brushed against him.

Temporary. The word would be his mantra while he was here. But he'd given his friend a vow that he would address his past, and that meant returning as Lord of Mei Solis. That meant providing income, checking the buildings and the gates and the houses. And it also meant meeting with tenants and attending councils.

With Matilda now in the room, he sat. He rolled his shoulders again, feeling the tightness there. He looked at his childhood friends and they looked steadily at him.

Pretending to be Lord of the Manor had never sat well with him. It was a title that his father had coveted and derived pleasure from. His grandfather, a harsh man, had liked to hold power over others. He was the one who had grown the acreage and the tenancy. Who'd had the ambition to obtain other manors and gain a title, to give tithes to the King.

However, though it was what was considered a 'minor' manor, Mei Solis had more substance than that. The tenants were close to a hundred and the acreage was almost a thousand. The land was certainly vast enough for two, if not three manors, but his grandfather had had grander schemes than that. And he'd ordered the size of Mei Solis to be much larger than most minor manors. An entire village might find residence inside.

And that was one of the problems. The acreage was vast enough to earn a large income. But the size of Mei Solis required huge funds for upkeep, and then the King's wars required more in from its vassals.

His father had had to travel to gain coin, but that had required him to leave his land.

For most of those years Nicholas had been training at Edward's court. Unfortunately his father had left the manor in the hands of one bad steward after another. His father had also been poor at making decisions that would benefit.

Mei Solis had fallen into ruin.

Nicholas had no ambition for multiple manors, like his grandfather. He also had no need for the power behind the title, like his father. Anything larger than this one manor had never been his dream. One home was enough, and on many days even that was unwanted. At one point he'd dreamed of something grand for Matilda, but that dream was dead.

All he could do for his future was find some semblance of peace—like Rhain—and try to protect his back.

Six years as a mercenary and he had garnered many enemies—but none so powerful as the Warstone family. And, much as his personal matters needed attending to, he had other duties.

Now that he had crossed paths, if not swords, with the Warstone family, he fully intended to tighten his ties with the King for protection. Not only for himself but for the manor, and for the mercenaries he travelled with. And that meant increasing tithes to the King.

What he did here for the next few months needed to have a lasting effect. In that time he would pretend he was a lord with multiple manors, like some of the men he'd met. They never stayed on one estate for long.

He stood up. 'I want to give you my appreciation for the years you have served this land and my home.'

Louve raised his brow. 'Are you intending on usurping us?'

The prospect was not even tempting, since he'd have to govern a piece of property that had never been his home. He'd do what needed to be done here and then leave.

'Of course. The manor is falling into ruin and I've obviously arrived just in time,' he said sarcastically, and sat down again.'

'He is definitely intending to usurp us,' Louve said, his eyes on Matilda.

Her eyes stayed wary, but the curve of her lips eased at the joke was shared between them. The two of them shared a commonality, and he was the odd one out.

But there was one long-time joke that had once been shared amongst them all: his lack of interest in the crops and the land. He had only taken the reins of the plough when his father had died. A moment when Fate had showed him that his feeble efforts at major operations weren't enough to feed his tenants and to provide for Matilda as he'd wanted to.

'I can assure you, you are safe with your duties.'

Louve's eyes returned to his, the merriment dimmed despite Nicholas's attempt at continuing the laughter. 'Why don't I feel secure with your statement?'

'Because he's called a council between us. When has he *ever* held a meeting?' Matilda quipped.

Not even when he'd left. He'd simply stood in a field one day, they had already been there, and he'd said it. That he was leaving in a week to earn the coin necessary to pay for the roof that had fallen.

A week during which he and Matilda— *No.* He wouldn't think of those days. Never again.

He glanced at Matilda. Quiet when she never had been before. Whenever they'd talked it had always been she who had interjected. Her restlessness had made her never one for polite or formal means of conversation. But now Matilda remained quiet, her arms around her belly, her hands in her lap, her eyes bouncing from him to Louve.

'I've called a meeting because I've been gone for six years and I don't know a damn thing about what's been going on.'

Matilda's eyes caught his.

Was she surprised that he could admit to a fault?

'Not even two full days here and you are disparaging my reports to you,' Louve said.

'I doubt I received all the correspondence you sent. I only received the more...*choice* letters.'

His friendship with Louve was mended, but Nicholas couldn't fathom making peace with Matilda. Matilda's expression when she looked at him was mutinous.

'So what do you want to know?' Louve said.

He'd received some correspondence, so he knew how things had been when Roger was still alive, but now...?

'Tell me how matters are operated here.'

'We have the tenants working your demesne two days a week, their own the rest,' Louve said. 'I keep track with tally sticks. The tenants understand them when I make the notches.'

Nicholas nodded. 'How to increase production?'

'How much silver did you bring?' Matilda said.

Even Louve swung his gaze to her at that.

Avarice. Greed. He'd never attributed those things to Matilda, only to Helena. Still, he'd wanted to give her riches. Told her he'd leave to bring them home to her.

But he'd been gone a long time, and perhaps with the silver he had sent home she had grown greedy.

'Enough for lifetimes,' he replied.

Louve darted another look to Matilda and replied, 'Then we can get the tools we need. We can hire people to help with the bleeding of the livestock and the storage of the wheat we've harvested. We've lost some of our crops simply because there aren't been enough people to get it into shelter.'

'Or enough shelters,' Matilda added. 'When

we go out you'll see some of the buildings we've constructed, but the crops have yielded more and we have no storage.'

'Then let's do it,' he replied. All that would increase his tithes to the King. Everything sounded as if it was running smoothly.

'The manor's roof has been repaired. The walls and floors have been reinforced,' Matilda added. 'As you instructed.'

Louve shot her another puzzled glance. 'Fortifications, too, were reinforced. Everything I wrote to you about.'

Everything seemed too easy. When he had been here, when his father had been Lord, crops hadn't yielded so much that storage had been needed. Tenants had not worked the land.

'And how are the disputes? Surely there must be disputes?'

'What can't be resolved we hold council meetings for,' Louve interjected. 'At the beginning there were many.'

'All three of you?'

'At the beginning,' Louve said. 'Then I left matters to Roger and Matilda.'

He could imagine them now, sitting side by side, the Lord and Lady of the manor.

'And now?'

'There has been no council for some time.'

'Disputes?'

'Too many,' Louve quipped. 'But with—

'I will attend these meetings.' Nicholas turned to Louve. 'Then you can supervise the planting of the barley without interruption.'

Louve's tapping fingers stopped. Nicholas saw a brief flare in Matilda's eyes. But then it was gone, and she put a hand to her belly.

Louve's eyes went from Matilda to Nicholas. 'Don't you think I should attend?'

'It is most expedient that I know the affairs of my tenants. There are many I have not talked to.'

He waited for her reaction. After all, he intended to sit by her side as they should have done all those years ago.

But Matilda said nothing. No one protested.

Nicholas stretched back in the chair as if he hadn't a care in all the kingdom, but suddenly he felt weighed down with them all.

Chapter Eight

The baby kicked again, and Matilda stood. 'Is this better?' she whispered. 'Is this what you want?'

'Who are you talking to?' Agnes came bounding in.

As always, Agnes's hair was coming undone from her plaits and her clothes were haphazardly put on.

'I'm talking to the baby.'

The young girl's brows drew in. 'Can she hear you?'

Matilda almost smiled. She had everyone except Rohesia, Louve and Bess believing that the baby would be a girl. A few more weeks and they'd know she was right.

'I don't know, but if she can is there something you'd like to say to her?'

Agnes's eye grew as big as full moons and she hastily shook her head.

'Not even a little bit?'

'There's so much!' Agnes blurted. 'She hasn't seen the horses, or the fields. Nor the new linens in the hall or how Cook's makes her raston bread sweet for you.'

Oh, to see the world through a child's eyes. A world where everything was of equal importance.

'Maybe you don't have to tell her all that. Maybe you could simply tell her a secret message?'

'Can I touch your belly?'

At Matilda's nod, Agnes laid her small hand gently on her stomach.

Matilda gasped.

Agnes quickly stepped back. 'Did I hurt you?'

She shook her head. 'Your hand is cold, that's all. Do you have enough clothing on under that cloak? It is unseasonably chilly for September.'

With a shy grin, Agnes shrugged.

Agnes was always either half-dressed or hardly fed. Her mind was usually occupied with the shape of a butterfly's wings or the way the water carved through mud. But the weather was turning, and despite the cloak Agnes's cheeks and nose were bright red and her hands were like ice.

'How long have you been outside?'

'Not long.'

Which could mean hours. 'Did you leave the house before or after breakfast?'

'Before, I think.'

Definitely hours. 'Why don't you talk to the baby and I'll make you some pottage?'

Agnes nodded eagerly and placed her hand on her belly again. She leaned in and whispered, 'Can't wait to play with you.'

Matilda, who was trying to keep her sudden happy tears at bay, said, 'She can't wait to play with you either.'

Agnes clasped her hands. 'Did she tell you that?'

'No, but I know *I* can't wait to play with you, so it makes sense that she can't either.'

Agnes clapped, her whole body vibrating.

'What are you building today?' asked Matilda.

'Wolves.'

'Wolves? But what will happen to the horses that you built the other day?'

'They're circling the barns.'

It was quite a story. 'Where is this one built?'

'In the herb garden.'

Her brothers wouldn't think of entering the garden. 'But how can you build anything there?' The stalks of the vegetables and herbs would surely impede any structures.

'It's only some rocks and sticks on the ground.'

Matilda's heart panged. Though most of them fell down, Agnes liked to stack things on top of each other.

Agnes nodded. 'Maybe the baby could help me when she gets out.'

'It'll be a while before she can play with you in that way. I'm afraid she might be more like your brothers at first, and destroy your creations before you can blink.'

'Is Agnes here?' Bess called.

'In here,' Matilda answered.

Bess strode in. 'Your mother's looking for you.'

'I'm fine in here,' Agnes said.

'I'm about to feed her,' Matilda added, walking to the pot by the fire. Not hot, but warm enough. She placed the pottage in a cup and Agnes wrapped her hands around it.

'What brings you here?' Matilda asked Bess.

Bess poured herself some pottage and sat down. 'Rohesia's wondering where you are.'

'You're running messages today?'

'It appears so.' Bess took a sip.

'Why does Rohesia want me?'

'Apparently, you've been having pains.'

'When I'm bending over—you know of those.'

But there were also those pains she'd experienced in the middle of the night, when she was lying down, and the other ones when she was standing. She'd never mentioned them. Didn't want to worry anyone.

Bess gave her a sideways glance.

'You don't have to believe me.'

Bess opened her mouth closed it. Opened it again. 'You never tell me everything.'

'We've known each other since I was a babe—what more is there to say?'

Bess turned to Agnes. 'Ready to return? Let's walk back to your house.'

Handing the cup over, Agnes frowned. 'I know my way!'

'You may know your way, but I said I'd get you home,' Bess said.

'And I have to leave, too.' Matilda swung on her cape which caught on her belly. Giggling, Agnes straightened it out, while Bess opened the door and they stepped out.

Agnes skipped ahead of them.

'What's the true reason Rohesia wants to see me?'

Bess shrugged. 'That's all she said. You know what's she like—mixing those herbs and bending over her cauldrons, plotting.'

She wanted to say that Rohesia didn't plot, but she had watched them all grow into adults. The healer did plot, and she nudged until a person had no choice left.

They passed Agnes's home and she ran inside, waving goodbye.

'That child thinks you walk on silver,' Bess said. 'All those drawings in the sand and the little piles of rocks and sticks. You spend too much time with her.'

'It'll be good practice for me and her mother needs a break.'

'But all those *things* she builds. I'm constantly tripping over them. Nuisances.'

'To her they're wolves and horses.'

'Maybe they'd look like that to me if I had enough ale, but they're simply sticks that need to be turned into kindling.'

'You're terrible!' Matilda laughed. 'And that's very untrue. I wish she could have teaching from someone who does such things.'

Bess laughed. 'Mei Solis could never afford a resident artist.'

'We can be a poor patron and only provide food and ale.'

'More like day-old bread and water. Plus, after that disaster Agnes created before, you'll want someone who is truly trained. Not someone who says they can do it only to get fed.'

'I truly thought that wattle and daub would work.'

Bess laughed. 'Everyone thought you were up to your old tricks again.'

'They were supposed to walk *around* it.'

'She built everything right at the entrance. There was no going *around* anything. And when it all collapsed the mixture stuck to cart wheels and horses hooves.'

Matilda's only care had been the crestfallen look on Agnes's face. And now, with a few more crops like the last one and the sheep continuing to grow, they'd soon have enough for someone.

Bess shook her head. 'Your carving only encourages her.'

'Those horses on the manor's stones? I did that years ago.'

Bess gave her a look.

'What is it?'

'If you don't want to notice, why should the rest of us tell you?' Bess quipped. 'Looks like Rohesia is inside.'

Great billowing puffs of smoke were pouring out through the only vent.

Matilda's heart clenched. 'Where's my father?'

With a shared look, they rushed forward.

'What's happening over there?' Nicholas asked.

'Thought you'd like the look of that,' Louve said. 'New buildings—but the best view is if you go through them.'

A sound stopped them. A screeching that was above the animals' cries and the squeals of children. To Nicholas it sounded like the frantic calls of women whose homes were getting ransacked.

Louve didn't seem concerned, but there was something wrong here.

'What is that?' he asked.

Louve looked grim. 'You'll see soon enough.'

Though it had been a long time, he knew the direction in which they went. He'd know the way if he'd lost *both* eyes.

Matilda's house.

There had been a time when he'd counted the steps to her front door. Just for fun. Just because the weather had been bad and he'd had the time. And he'd wanted to know—to boast to her that though his home was farther away than Louve's or Roger's it took him less steps because he was bigger and better than them.

More importantly, he remembered the day the number had become less. When he'd grown up and he hadn't needed as many steps to reach her. That was the day he'd realised that his heart needed more beats. The day he'd wanted not only to play with her and tease her, but to kiss her, too.

They took another turn. The noise wasn't coming from Matilda's old home, but the healer's. A small girl was hovering outside the doorway.

He could hear them now. Voices that were familiar. Bess, Matilda, her father. But her father's voice was different...overwrought.

'Get him out of here!' Rohesia screeched. 'Out! I'll have to start all over again and—

'Come on, Father. Step back,' Matilda coaxed.

'Fire!'

'It's Rohesia's fire,' Matilda said.

'He's worse. I'm telling you he's worse. He needs more than me!' shouted Rohesia.

'Just a bit more storing the grain and planting the barley. Only a fortnight or two.'

'He'll catch on fire by then. Even now I wonder if I have enough dried herbs!'

Nicholas looked behind him. Louve was escorting the little girl in the opposite direction. He hurried to the door and took in the scene before him. Rohesia—tiny, bent, her hair so grey and thin it was almost non-existent—waved a spoon like a vengeful sprite.

Matilda, her tall frame encumbered by her pregnancy, had her hands against an older man's arms and was turning him. When they shuffled around to face the doorway, Nicholas almost gasped. *Holgar.* Matilda's father. The man had stood almost as tall as him the last time he'd seen him. Holgar had shaken his hand and wished him a profitable journey when his daughter had not.

Then his gaze met Matilda's, and he noticed nothing else.

Nicholas was at the door. His eyes were wide, uncomprehending. Taking in everything. Her father trembled underneath her hands. Fragile not just in body, but in his mind. Rohesia, who needed care herself, was still shrieking, making her father's frantic whispers worse. And there was she, with her swollen belly, her painful hips, her worry.

She didn't want this man to see her like this. 'What are you doing here?'

Matilda was so stunned to see him she didn't realise her father was taking a trembling step without support. When he stumbled, it was Nicholas who rushed up to provide a steadying hand. Matilda was so shocked she allowed it.

'Nicholas, you've returned,' Holgar said.

Absolute. Silence.

'I have.'

Holgar patted Nicholas's hand. 'Get me home, then. I'm tired.'

'I'll do it,' Matilda said.

Holgar looked at his daughter. 'You're good, Matilda.'

Her heart stopped and wouldn't start. It wouldn't. And it was almost impossible to get words out. But it was a couple of days since the last time her father had talked, and she wouldn't miss this opportunity now.

'I'll get you home,' she said.

Holgar looked to Nicholas. '*Good* Matilda.'

Nicholas's brow drew in and a muscle popped in his jaw. 'That she is.'

'Joan was always cold...'

'She was,' Matilda said. Her mother had constantly stretched her hands and feet to the fire, even in summer. Now her father seemed determined to put all fires out.

Slowly they walked him to the door. Her father's words made her heart soar, but Nicholas's presence did not.

Behind them, Rohesia lowered her spoon. 'Does this mean I'll get finer flour?'

'If there is any,' Matilda called back.

'I'll ensure it.' Nicholas's voice rang through the tiny hut at the same time.

Matilda didn't care for the authority behind Nicholas's words, nor his sentiment. Did he think he could fix this just because he'd returned? He didn't deserve to repair this private part of her life. He wasn't—had chosen not to be—family.

Her father gained his footing and she released his arm to get his own door open. Just a few short steps and they were inside. Stable enough, Holgar let go of Nicholas as well.

'You can go now,' she said as her father sat.

The fire was no more than embers. She'd build it, and then he could stretch his own hands and feet to the heat.

There was silence as the door closed, but she knew Nicholas was still there.

'It's fine. I'll fix the fire, then some food,' she said.

'Are you tired, Holgar?' asked Nicholas.

'Always,' he said.

He asked. Her father answered. And she couldn't be sad about his response, for when would he go away again?

Fire done, she decided to just take this moment. Ever restless, Nicholas would leave soon enough. Taking her father's hand, she sat down next to her father and stared at the flames.

'What can I do?' whispered Nicholas.

'There's vegetables in the bucket by the door. Bess brought them earlier, to make soup,' Holgar said.

Matilda squeezed her father's hand and laughed.

She'd get to making soup in a moment, when Nicholas had left.

But he didn't leave. Instead, soon the sound of the chopping of potatoes and turnips filled the air.

As her father regaled them with tales of his prowess in wooing her mother, she turned to look behind him.

Nicholas's back was to her, his head bowed to his task. She realised that the table was under the ceiling beams and he would probably crack the top of his head if he stood tall.

She watched the rhythmic way his shoulders and arms moved as he performed such a domestic task, the cradling of his large hands and long fingers as he shoved the chopped vegetables he'd done to one side before beginning again.

He was...*efficient* at it, which surprised her. The Nicholas of old wouldn't even have planted a vegetable. The lone time he had been in the fields after his father's death he had spent tearing through the soil.

A few more moments passed as he found a pan

and filled it with water. Then came the heavy tread of his boots as he walked it to the fire.

All the while she carried on listening to her father and tried to ignore the giant in the room.

When Nicholas was done, and had nestled the pot in the flames, Holgar turned to him. 'Will it poison me?'

'Do you want it to?'

Her father chuckled, but there was a strange look to his eyes now. Not lost or confused, but pained. She squeezed his hand and he, in turn, squeezed hers. She was certain that Nicholas would leave, but then her father began a conversation with him, so she didn't say anything.

She'd hold his hand and rest a little, for the sake of the baby growing in her womb. After the meal, her father would most likely need sleep and Nicholas would go. He needed to go. He was too big for this room and, despite his help, he didn't belong here with her and her father.

Yet she was loath to upset this moment of peace.

Except Nicholas did not share in this peace. His feet were apart, as if he was bracing himself against a storm or preparing for an attack. The fingers that had so effectively taken care of the vegetables were flexing at his sides, and even as he talked his jaw was tight.

His eyes actively refused to look her way. So she kept hers on him as they ate and conversed.

But through it all she could see Nicholas wasn't at peace at all, though he held himself still and took methodical mouthfuls of soup, though he talked with her father on matters of the past and about the time he was away.

He never avoided her father's questions, but he was always careful about what he said of his mercenary life. As for the tale of his lost eye— he said nothing at all.

When her father leaned back in his chair, his eyes slumberous, she stood. 'I'll clean up.'

Nicholas glanced to her then. His gaze was steady, as if he hadn't been avoiding looking at her, but she could read nothing in it.

'I'll do it,' he said.

Now wasn't the time to argue. With a nod, she helped her father up, but as she walked behind him, to follow him in the other room, her father patted her on the shoulder. 'Not tonight,' he said, and then he turned around.

Slowly, something sombre and dark surfaced in the room between all three of them. It was there in her father's searching eyes and in the tenor of Nicholas's reaction. It rose suddenly, as if it had been waiting and watching until this moment.

'You've returned,' Holgar said.

Her father's eyes roamed the room, rested on her, on her swollen belly. Then his eyes met hers. Her father was definitely here now. All the conversations they'd had since Nicholas had left were there in his eyes.

At first he had argued with her, told her to give it more time. But as months had gone by and no messages had come, when her mother had passed, they'd both wanted some joy.

When Roger had asked to marry her, her father had given his blessing. She'd always wondered if he'd had reservations about it, as she'd had. If the happiness they'd sought had ever been found.

'Less one eye, and with three times the coin I thought I'd have,' Nicholas replied.

'Was it worth the delay?' Holgar asked. 'Being late? Is this what you wanted?'

Nicholas's eyes slid to hers. 'It's what *she* wanted.'

There was a gleam to her father's eyes. 'As long as you understand that.'

On the way to his room, her father patted her shoulder. Still reeling from the exchanged words, she could only rest her hand on his. There had always been respect between her father and Nicholas, but she hadn't expected any concession or confession. And she wasn't certain if what she'd heard was either.

When she turned back, Nicholas was arranging the fire for the evening. Taking her cue from him, she placed their bowls and spoons on the table.

'Bess will come by in a few hours, and the cordwainer's wife before dawn,' she said, though he didn't deserve an explanation. 'We can go.'

She didn't know what to expect from his silence, but he held the door open and she brushed by him. The afternoon light was only just dying, and there were people about. They garnered a few looks, but she studiously avoided them. She'd learned that skill long ago.

'What's happened to him?'

For one blinding moment she didn't know what Nicholas meant. Her father had seemed to be back with them. Completely, forcefully and protectively back. His words still rang inside her, and she suspected in Nicholas as well.

But if things were as they had been for the last few years her father would soon get lost again. She wasn't so naive as to think that now Nicholas had returned her father would too.

'It is simply age, Nicholas. It's not your concern.'

He kept silent, but when they reached the fork in the road where he needed to turn towards his home and she to hers, he stayed beside her. She glanced over at him.

He kept his eyes steady on the road, but he spoke. 'You need to return. I'll walk you home.'

She needed rest, but she didn't need her empty home, which was more difficult to return to every day. With an empty waiting cradle and no husband.

But with certainty she didn't belong to this man, who had spent hours with her in a tiny cottage, chopping vegetables and telling stories. Not a man who had looked her father straight in the eye and agreed that he had returned too late. What did that even *mean*? Did he mean because of her marriage to Roger? She had married him because Nicholas no longer wanted her—it wouldn't have mattered what year he'd arrived.

'I know the way,' she said, as politely as she could. She didn't need him and, more importantly, she didn't trust him.

'Allow me,' he answered.

She'd allowed him since she and Bess had rescued her father from Rohesia. The old Matilda would have stopped and said a few curt words. Perhaps even created a scene in order to get her way. Now she wouldn't. He'd watched and waited all evening. Now it was her turn to remain quiet and let him reveal his own secrets. She had shown him too much of hers tonight.

'Louve wrote to me about your mother,' he said after a few more steps.

Letters. She didn't want to talk about letters. *She* would have written to him about her mother if she'd thought her letter would be received.

'I'm sorry,' he continued. 'She was very witty.'

It was from her mother that she'd obtained her own sense of humour and adventure. When her mother had died, it had been as if a light had gone out for her father and her. And when Nicholas hadn't written…

'Your words are a bit late, Nicholas, and I'm tired. What is it that you want to know?'

'Why is your father not with you?'

Those were not the words she'd expected, though she should have. Nicholas and her father had been close. A relationship perhaps born out of the fact that his own father had been obsessed with everything but his son.

However, her father and Roger's relationship had been different. Cordial, but with no special closeness. Recently she had become more worried for her father, but had seen no solution. Roger had loved his home, away from all the others, and it was only one room. The bed was next to the table. They'd have eventually built something for her father, but there had not been enough time…

'These matters are not your concern,' she said.

'The manor has room, with plenty of people and servants always nearby. As bailiff, you have every right to live there and to have your father do so.'

As his wife she'd have had even more right. 'He is in his home, where he wishes to remain,' she lied.

The manor *would* be a better place for him, but that wasn't an option she would even consider. It had taken a long time for her to be accepted as Roger's wife. And she wanted what was best for her baby. That meant she must keep the boundaries clear when it came to where she lived.

'It may be his wish, but is he capable?' Nicholas said.

She could hold her sense of patience only so long. 'You go too far to discuss this. As if you care. As if what I tell you matters. Because I know it doesn't. Not after—' She stopped, waved her hand. 'Not after all this time. I know you have other people to attend to, and I assure you I know my way home.'

'Who was that little girl?'

The change of subject didn't confuse her. Nicholas's mind had always worked like this. What she *didn't* like was how familiar it was, or the fact that she answered him.

'Outside the door?'

'I walked here with Louve, and there was a little girl with long curly hair, about this height. He took her away.'

There was a dull stab to her belly, and she stopped to rub it. 'She shouldn't have been there. We'd only just taken her home.'

Nicholas's eyes flicked to the movement of her hand, a question in his gaze.

'I'm fine,' she said, walking a bit slower.

'Who is she?' Nicholas asked after a few slow steps.

'Agnes. She's the cordwainer's daughter.'

'You know her well?'

'I know everyone well.' If he had stayed, he'd know them, too.

He looked away at that, but she saw a muscle tick in his jaw and knew he understood. 'She's close to you?'

She didn't know where these questions were coming from, or their purpose. Nevertheless, she *did* know that she didn't want to be walking to her home with the man who had broken her heart.

'She's a sweet, curious child. I'm glad Louve was here to return her to her parents.'

'Does she follow you around often?'

'Why all these questions?'

He stepped back. 'I've returned, Matilda. I'd like to know how my home has fared while I was gone.'

But these questions weren't about his home. They were personal and about her. She'd shared enough tonight. She'd done it for her father's sake, not for him.

'You never cared for this home. Even when your father slaved over it and brought home that woman. Even when your father worked himself to death. You didn't care. I'd go so far as to say you hated it.'

'I worked as hard as my father—while he was alive and after he died,' he said with deadly calm. 'When that wasn't enough I became a sword for hire. And you say, after all my sacrifices, after all I've lost, that I *hated* it?'

Yes! she wanted to answer. *Always, yes.* He had left not because of some love of the land but because he'd hated it. Because he had been restless, and building a life with her here hadn't been for him. It had only been some vow to his father, some promise to Helena, that had fuelled his drive to build up Mei Solis.

The same vow that had destroyed their relationship.

It had simply taken him not writing for her to realise it. The moment he'd left had been the moment he'd broken her heart. When she had known that they didn't have the same ideas on how they wanted their lives together to be.

Yet these were all old arguments—ones she hadn't thought she'd have to make ever again. She'd married another man so she could *stop* having these arguments.

'None of this mattered to you before,' she said.

'It'll matter to you less when you leave again.'

'I've just returned. What makes you believe I'll leave?'

'You always do.'

Chapter Nine

Silently walking down the steps the next morning, Nicholas still couldn't get Matilda's words out of head. And staring at the linen tapestries in his room all night had given him no answers as to why he'd stayed in Holgar's home as long as he had.

It had all started with a brief walk with Louve to show him more buildings. Then Rohesia's shrieking. Nothing new. Nicholas could see that now. No other neighbour had reacted because it was a common occurrence.

Nonetheless, Louve had hurried there and, as a result, so had he. Then Louve had left, taken that little girl and hadn't come back. He hadn't been concerned. Yet one step into Rohesia's home and Nicholas's feet hadn't moved again.

Rohesia had always been volatile and territorial. So he had been surprised to see Matilda and her father there with her. More than surprised to see the gentle, caring way Matilda had been trying to extract her father from the situation. The Matilda *he* knew would have said a few firm words to let her know where she stood.

This Matilda had been almost flustered, placating instead. Her behaviour had been incongruous in the woman he'd left behind. There had been strength there. She was no coward, but she acted as if she were timid.

The last time he'd seen Holgar the man had been almost double the weight he was now, and as proud as any king. Now he appeared diminished.

He knew Joan had died, but this kind of change seemed dramatic. It had wrenched something inside him to see the man reduced, because he was someone who had been there for him when his own father had died. Who had watched him grow and agreed he was a good match for his daughter.

Seeing him like that…

Nicholas shook his head and walked directly to the door leading out of the hall. He was grateful that the few people who were beginning their day weren't asking him questions or enquiring about his health. He'd had all night, but he still needed to sort his thoughts.

He had stayed though he'd had no right being in that house. No excuse. With Holgar there, he had known he wouldn't confront Matilda. He had stayed because for a moment Matilda had needed him to be there. To chop vegetables and listen to her father. To listen to her accusations and to Holgar and his words.

And that thought had driven a dagger right through his thoughts. Made his sleep restless and forced him up before dawn broke.

He had left all those years ago. They'd argued. He'd had to go because they'd needed coin. Because he had known his duty to his home, his vassals, his tenants. He had known his desire for her.

Yet, underneath it all, he did intend to leave again. How could he possibly stay here? Why would she and Louve want him to? They were doing an excellent job of running and improving Mei Solis. More than that, how had she guessed the truth?

He hated to think that she could still know him. Had she guessed that he wanted to confront his past in order to find peace? Despite her grief, she'd seemed to find it. Widowed, with a child on the way...

Holgar's words had been clear: respect Matilda's choices.

She'd chosen Roger while he had been out earning silver for her...for *them*. So they would have a house with a solid roof, oxen to furrow the land. So he didn't have to work to his death. So they could have children with stability.

He'd left, and at the moment when he had been earning everything they needed so they could be together she had betrayed him. How was he to respect or reconcile the past?

And yet he'd stayed for hours with Matilda and her father. He had no right thinking that she'd needed him there. Besides, remaining in one place and chopping vegetables went against everything in him.

If something needed to be done, he did it. Coin was needed— he became a mercenary and earned it. A friend killed a man in a reckless moment—he killed two to keep him alive.

He wanted to find peace and happiness—he returned here to find it.

Chopping vegetables had got him nowhere. He needed to confront her, to demand why she betrayed him.

However, after those hours locked in uncharacteristic quietness with her and her father, with her father's words still scraping uncomfortably within him, he knew he wouldn't. Not today. He was too reckless and restless for that. So that left…*what* for him to do?

He hadn't belonged here before he'd left, and he didn't belong here now. He didn't recognise anything or anyone. This wasn't the home he'd left, or the people. He wouldn't stay here, but he needed a future. One in which whatever still thumped in his heart when he looked at Matilda, whatever rage he felt towards Roger, was gone. A new home, new friends, a woman who would truly trust him.

He refused to spend the rest of his life looking over his shoulder, waiting for Reynold to attack. And to do so he needed to make Mei Solis so prosperous that the King couldn't do without its tithes.

Did he regret what Rhain had done that night when he'd made the deal with Reynold? *No.* Rhain made that deal with Reynold to protect Helissent. Someone he loved had been at risk, and he'd have made any bargain with the devil. Rhain had protected his future. Now Nicholas would ensure *he* could have a future as well. And he was eager to begin it.

Nicholas strode through the courtyard towards the stables. He was so restless he could probably walk to the outer fields.

His land.

In the days he'd spent here he'd already ridden through much of the land. And there was more to cover at this time of year, with many of the outer fields just harvested.

He had a large estate, but it was worthless unless the land was used. Over his travels he'd seen different farming styles. But, though he wanted to adopt some of the techniques he'd seen in Spain, he knew most would be useless in this climate. Most, but not all.

'I can't get the tail right!' Agnes cried, her voice too full of happiness for her complaint to have any real bearing.

'Well, look at this back leg I have drawn—what horse ever had a leg like that?' Matilda pointed to the ground, where they were scraping sticks in the dirt.

Laughing, Agnes skipped around it. 'It looks like a dog.'

Matilda took a large step back to look at their work, and was rewarded with a jab in her side and along her left leg. She froze.

Agnes stopped skipping. 'Is she talking again?'

Matilda waited a moment before she could reply. 'Very loudly.'

'Can I listen?'

Matilda breathed out slowly until the pain had eased. She shouldn't have stepped back so quickly. 'Always.'

'Are you well?' Agnes whispered to the baby.

Another pang. 'I think… *Oh!*' Matilda's hand went to her belly.

'Is she kicking again?' Agnes asked.

A short walk and they'd be at the edge of the village. By then someone would surely have crossed their path.

'Why don't we go and see if Rohesia is near?'

Agnes bit her lip. Matilda grabbed the girl's hand and gave her a smile, but she could feel her body tightening. Readying, and yet she wasn't ready. It was too soon for her baby's arrival; she hadn't enough clothes sewn.

A few more steps and they did run into some-one—but it wasn't Rohesia or Bess. It was Nich-olas, striding over from the cordwainer's. They were still on his blind side, and Matilda hoped that he would continue, but it was a foolish hope. He never appeared to *have* a blind side when it came to her. His gaze always found hers.

She couldn't straighten, and a sheen of sweat broke out on her skin, but she loosened her grip on Agnes and tried to appear as if all was well as she smiled.

Whatever Nicholas saw in her expression hastened his steps to her. 'What has happened?'

'The baby's coming,' Agnes said.

'She's not!' Matilda said. 'I stood too quickly and have a pang in my side. I simply need to lie down and rest.'

'Rest?' Nicholas asked.

Wrong word. How many times had she argued that she didn't *need* to rest? 'Stretch a bit. She doesn't like it when I hunch over and don't give her space to move.'

'You've gone pale,' Nicholas said, looking around. There was still no one. 'Find Bess and Rohesia,' he said to Agnes. 'Tell them to meet us at the manor.'

Spinning on her heels, Agnes didn't wait for Matilda's response.

'I don't need to go to the manor!' Another sharp pain, but it was still only uncomfortable. 'I want to go home.'

Nicholas's eyes narrowed. 'I have already told Agnes where to go. Bess and Rohesia won't go to your home.'

'This is too much. It was probably only something I ate that didn't—' There was a flash between her legs. Hot…wet. 'My waters—' Matilda gripped her belly.

Nicholas cursed as he gripped her for support. 'Stop arguing.'

'Rohesia says a first child always takes its time. We can make it back to my home.'

At that moment Nicholas wasn't certain who would make it where…or how. He'd certainly seen worse in his travels—been assaulted by more chaos and confusion than one woman giving birth. Nevertheless, this was Matilda. *His* Matilda. And, for better or worse, he was the only one here to provide support, to get her to help. To *give* her help.

Yet with her grip on his arm he couldn't move. There was a vulnerability within her at this moment they shared that made his chest burn.

He offered Matilda his other arm and her fingers gripped so tightly he felt her fear through his cloak and his tunic, down to his very bones. Her trembles ensured that her worry vibrated through the rest of his body and every bit of the vicinity around his heart.

Looking at her determined expression, he couldn't guess what was happening to her, but her trembles told him they'd never make it out of the village.

'I don't want to go to the manor,' Matilda repeated. 'I need—' A sharp inhalation. 'I need to go to my home. The cradle is there, as are all the linens. I have prepared it for this.'

'Your home is too far for you to make it.' Nicholas indicated with his chin. 'You're gathering attention. Do you want that?'

Now everyone had decided to appear? She shook her head. 'This is—'

'What is necessary,' he interrupted. 'If you don't agree, I will carry you.'

She frowned at him, and a pang cut through his chest as a memory clashed with the present. How familiar she was in this moment, with her hazel eyes flashing at him. How many times had they stood toe to toe like this in the past, until their childhood dirt clods had turned to kisses?

Those kisses had burned through him all those three years until he'd received her letter. They burned through him now.

Exhaling, he shook his head. There was no time for the past when she needed him so much now.

She shuffled forward, but stopped short of a full stride. One hand on him, the other on her baby. 'I think I may have got my wish.'

'What was that?'

'That she'd come early.'

Nicholas cursed, then swept her up. Her cloak, her heavy skirts, the weight of her pregnancy.

He felt none of it. The rush of her smell, like the soil before it rained and fresh spring grass, was what almost brought him to his knees.

She was grasping behind his neck and he felt the trusting weight of her, the fact that she fitted so comfortably in his arms—as if she belonged. He didn't know who was more vulnerable at that moment—he in the flash of memories of things that would never happen again between them, or her because of the babe that was to come.

The baby. Usually women were confined before this happened. Not out in the open, exposed to people, edging closer, their eyes wide with worry.

She shouldn't be exposed to *him*.

Her breath sped. She was suddenly pale, then red. Her entire body tensed against the coming contraction.

'Nicholas!'

'I won't drop you.'

Her eyes met his, and all the years fell away.

'I know,' she said.

He'd never wanted to reach his home before. Not with this urgency and absolute need. Now it was his sole desire. Rushing through the gates into the courtyard, he demanded linens, water, food and rushes to be sent to the room next to his.

Nicholas pushed by the crowds beginning to form. His vision of Matilda was marred by the patch over his eye. He'd have to look down to see her and he forced himself not to.

She was too close. He held her too tightly. But she clung just as much as her pain came and went, as her hands fluttered from his neck to her belly. He sensed her struggle. This moment was all for the baby—but she, the mother, had to get somewhere safe first.

He bounded up the steps, past his room, to the chamber that adjoined it. The one he'd been sleeping in to avoid what she had done to the master chamber.

'Here?' she said.

'You heard my shouting.'

'I'm in pain—I'm hardly listening to *you*.'

Already servants were passing him, pushing open the door. 'Well, you should be.'

He took her to the bed to lie her down.

'I want to stand.'

He eased her down. Her trembles were increasing as her legs took her weight, as another wave of pain swept through her.

She gripped his arm again. 'Bess and Rohesia will be here soon.'

'I need to walk.'

'Then we will walk.'

He could do nothing else. His heart was thumping and his limbs were heavy and clumsy next to hers. This wasn't some enemy he could fight. There was no tea or tincture to make this go away.

Women died from childbirth. Matilda might

be dying now. But her grip stung and the light in her eyes was undefeated. She wanted to walk, so they would walk until their feet pained, until the baby came. They would walk.

More servants…most ignoring them. One dropped the linens when she saw him.

Flushed red, bent over, Matilda almost laughed. 'You have to go.'

'I'm staying.'

'No man is allowed during this time.'

'I'm staying,' he repeated.

Her breath was speeding up again. She was gripping his arm, gripping her skirts. He leaned in to support her and she took his support, rubbing her forehead against his chest, against his heart. He laid a hand on the back of her neck. It was burning.

When the pain had subsided he shuffled them towards a bucket, relished the coolness of the water, dipped a washcloth and placed it on her neck.

'*Now* you decide to stay…' she whispered, with a different tone. Gratefulness?

'I'm not leaving you like this.'

She pushed against his chest. 'More walking, then.'

The room was large enough to make a slow side turn, but not long enough to get a good stretch if that was what she needed. 'We would be better in the hall.'

A grunt from her. 'I don't think so. I want to be private. We stay here.'

Her pain was increasing. Although he could tell, he couldn't imagine what she was going through. 'I'm not certain this room is enough.'

'All of this is enough,' she said.

Did that mean *he* was enough?

The door burst open and Rohesia and Bess stamped in. Bess swept to Matilda's side, her manner gentle, comforting.

Rohesia, looking like a mighty harridan from the old tales demanded, 'Out!'

Matilda didn't let him step away. Instead she gripped his arm with both her hands. Her pain was coming again.

'I'm staying,' he said.

Bess rubbed Matilda's back. 'We're here now. *You* shouldn't be.'

Matilda clenched his arm; he wasn't about to pass her off like some satchel.

'The baby's coming,' Bess said. 'You can't be here. Not even a husband would be allowed.'

He didn't care for the custom. What husband would *not* be in this room? He could do nothing for her, but if she wanted to walk, if she wanted to use his arm for support and dig her nails in until his limb was numb…he could do that.

'She needs me.'

'I swear before God, you're not allowed to see this,' Rohesia barked. 'You're harming her by staying.'

'When all this is done she won't want you here,' Bess said more quietly. 'You're not her husband.'

Not her husband. Not his wife. He had never felt it more than now. Because if he was…if *she* was…he'd defy custom *and* God to be by her side.

He kept his gaze on Matilda's. Her face was flushed red, sweat dripping from her temples. Her breath came in short gasps with her cries of pain.

He had demanded to stay. God, the midwife and society demanded he go. As far as he was concerned only one person in this room had the right to make the decision.

'Matilda, do you want me here?'

She licked her lips, took a few quick breaths.

He bent at the knee to keep her face in his sight. Bess and Rohesia had backed away from them and he saw nothing else but her.

'Do you want me here?' he asked again.

She kept her eyes on him. Showed all her emotions. And, wanting to take them away, to share them, he absorbed every one of them until his heart was no longer his own.

He waited.

'Yes,' she said, as if answering the question in his own soul. Yes, she'd allow him to share the burden, the pain and the joy to come. Yes, she'd allow him to be in this room and defy custom and God.

Kneeling before her, he took her hands. 'Then I'll stay.'

She squeezed his fingers—not in pain, but in comfort. 'Only until—'

Suddenly she ripped her hand away, walked around the bed.

Nicholas stood. 'Matilda…'

'She'll need to squat soon,' Rohesia said, scrubbing her hands and arms in the buckets near the fire.

Matilda put her hand to her belly. 'A few more moments yet.'

To see her like this, strong in her vulnerability, he had no doubts of his heart—he had no doubts of her. There were words to be spoken, but today was not that day. Today he was there if she wanted him.

She walked around the bed again, and then took his arm. He put the other arm around her waist.

'Walk with me until it's time, and then go.'

Her lips parted and cracked. He swiped the cup from the table. She laid her hands on his as he gave her watered ale. Slowly he lowered the cup, watched as her breaths sped again.

Not his place, not his wife, but he wanted to be here—and by some miracle she wanted him here.

Bess and Rohesia stayed out of the way. As the

sun fell, and the shadows in the room changed, Bess took to sewing, Rohesia to resting.

He walked with Matilda, gave her comfort, his strength, whatever she needed. Few words were exchanged. Few were needed.

All the time he'd spent here—all of it came to this.

'It's time!' Matilda cried out.

She released his arm, and blood rushed to the limb again. What else could he do? He wasn't a midwife. He knew no man was allowed in the birthing chamber. Yet everything inside him demanded to stay by her side. His unsteady legs and even more vulnerable heart were unable to work properly because *she* hurt.

Stepping past Bess and Rohesia, he gazed at Matilda, who sat with her head tilted down as the pain inside her eased. He brushed back her damp hair and looked into her hazel eyes. He could see everything there. And there was so much.

'The baby will come,' he told her, as if it were a vow. 'You will both be well.

He had never moved more slowly, reluctant

to leave her side. This wasn't right—it wasn't. Custom and God said he shouldn't have stayed even *this* long. But Matilda had asked him to stay and he was realising that he'd fight God to stay by her side.

'Come back,' she said. 'When the baby's swaddled, come back.'

Opening the door, he turned to hold her faltering gaze. 'I will.'

Striding down the hallway to the stairs, Nicholas shook his throbbing arm. He should be glad to be out of there, but he felt only loss. Of what? There were too many contradictions inside him.

Nothing was resolved between them, and perhaps it never would be. He could bury his past, and yet he couldn't see clearly enough to understand what he was feeling. Did he hate her or love her? Why had he demanded to stay?

He had been betrayed. Rejected by this woman in the harshest way. Nonetheless, everything in him knew it didn't matter. She had trusted him to bring her here, showed herself at her most vulnerable.

The Great Hall was filled with excited chatter, but it did nothing to drown out the cries up-stairs. He didn't make it down the steps before Louve came striding in.

Nicholas didn't appreciate the excitement, nor the candied almonds and other confections grac-ing the tables in celebration. However, he *was* grateful for Louve's appearance.

'Let's walk outside,' he said.

'What do you want to do? Look at the new gates?'

'You think I'll leave?' Nicholas asked, not hid-ing the bite behind his words. He couldn't stay here—not with the past the way it was, not with the future and no Matilda. He had to find an-other future for himself. It couldn't be here, and yet everyone expected him to stay.

Startled, Louve stepped back. 'I meant no harm.'

'Then why do you talk of the gates?'

'Because we've talked of everything else ex-cept for Spain and how you lost your eye.'

'And what about the gates?'

'They were paid for by your Spanish coin.'

'You think this will lead the conversation to talk of where I lost my eye?'

'Would you rather talk of Matilda? No, I thought not. Let's go for this walk you want.'

Another cry came from upstairs and their heads swivelled in the direction of the sound of distress.

Nicholas shared a look with Louve.

'She's strong,' Louve said.

'We'll stay in the courtyard,' Nicholas said. Away from the celebrations, but close enough for any news.

Outside, the air was cold. The day was turning to night. No sooner was he outside than he wished to be inside again. But there was no distraction there—only a future he imagined that he could not bury.

'Tell me about the gates,' Nicholas said.

'The gates?'

'Rather an excessive use of my coin, given we aren't near any coast and have no warring neighbours.'

'I didn't know what you'd be bringing home with you when you came.'

'What I'd be bringing home?'

'Mercenary bands or some enemy after you.'

'But only I arrived.'

'A disappointment—but your missing eye provided entertainment.'

He wanted to laugh. It was Louve's gift to make upheaval appear normal. However, he recognised the clever change in the conversation.

'You won't get the story,' Nicholas said. 'Not today.'

'It would provide distraction.'

'The gates are enough for now.'

'Because at any moment a band of mercenaries or the enemy will be riding through?'

'Not likely,' Nicholas scoffed.

No gate would hold back his enemy, Reynold, and he couldn't shake the vague sense of unease that Reynold would search for him here. Why he would, he didn't know. However, a man that powerful didn't let anyone who crossed him live a peaceful life.

'No mercenaries, no enemy...' Louve said, his eyes darting over his features. 'I wonder on that...'

Louve's observational skills hadn't diminished. He had always been the better huntsmen out of all of them. But Nicholas didn't need him to be hunting and finding his secrets. He'd promised Rhain he'd stay the winter. He was beginning to realise how difficult that would be.

Too many ghosts. Too many regrets and memories.

He'd left for a reason and not simply for the coin to be earned.

Nicholas shrugged a shoulder. 'There's no reason for such a visit. The group disbanded. Some went up to Edward's camp, the others I left in London when I travelled here.'

'So you were not alone with all our coin?'

'Worried for the coin?'

Louve nodded. 'Of course. One man to defend wealth like that? I like having the command of the purse, of building and making costly changes.'

'To a home that belongs to someone else?'

'Too true.'

Now that he could see all Louve's accomplishments he understood his lack of ambition even less. Louve excelled at maintaining the manor. He was exceptional on budgeting to make the changes.

Louve wasn't a knight, but he was as skilled as one. He wasn't rich, but he wasn't a pauper, and long ago he'd bought his own land. He should be running his own estate, or at least his own farmstead. He had women chasing him and yet he'd never married.

A recurring thought kept pricking at him. 'I gave you the responsibility intending to return within two years.'

'And you didn't. But I kept my responsibilities and stayed.' Louve held up his hands. 'I made my position clear in my letters. You knew where Matilda and Roger stood, too.'

He had known. However, returning here was getting under his skin. He understood Louve and Roger more. And Matilda— It wouldn't do to think of Matilda.

'You didn't need to stay,' Nicholas said. 'I would never have trapped you here.'

'You think I felt trapped?'

How could he not have? He didn't sound it, and yet there was no reason for him to have stayed.

'You mentioned a widow in your letters…'

'Mary.'

'Is she still…?'

Louve's eyes softened. 'I'm still lying with her, and eating her food when she invites me.' He sighed. 'I love her, if that's what you are asking.'

That surprised him. Louve had mentioned her, but said nothing of love. When he had wondered why Louve stayed he'd wondered if it was for her. Louve's confession now proved his guess right, but still…

'But you won't marry her?'

'She won't—

'It's a girl!' Bess shouted out of the window.

Nicholas bounded up the staircase.

Chapter Ten

The storm had battered the manor since dawn.
Now it was the afternoon, and Nicholas had
hoped it would end, but it was relentless. The
manor was quiet, all the work inside completed.
The weather outside impeded everything but the
most critical of outdoor tasks regarding the livestock and horses. He'd been with Louve, secur-
ing the animals until everything and everyone
was covered in mud.

Louve had escaped to Mary's, so he knew he'd
have no one to while away the evening with
warmed ale or wine by the fire in the Great Hall.

So his feet had brought him up to his own
room, which he'd been avoiding. Avoiding because Matilda was still in the adjoining room,

though he hadn't seen her since he'd brought her here instead of taking her to her own home.

For almost three weeks Matilda had hidden herself in that room. Food was brought in, but most was taken out uneaten. If she used the garderobe down the passage, he had never seen her.

The baby, Julianna, was there too, and he heard her cries. They were infrequent—most likely because Matilda was holding her and caring for her every need.

Every day Rohesia and Bess came. Gave soft knocks on the door, opened it though no one answered. Sometimes he saw them take the sleeping baby down the corridor to walk around the manor, or bundled her up for a trip outside. Some days Agnes would be with them.

Matilda was in still in his private rooms. Rooms she'd made homely in his absence. Rooms to recover from childbirth. But she'd been there overly long.

He'd heard Rohesia and Bess talking. The servants whispering. It was as if the arrival of her daughter had heralded the return of her grief for

Roger. At least that was the fear. That she was not progressing as a new mother should.

He, no doubt, was someone she didn't want to see. More, he had no right to go into that room. She was not his wife or sister. Not even, he was mostly sure, a friend.

He had a whole list of reasons not to go in there, though it had been weeks and she wasn't eating. Weeks and he wasn't certain whether the room was too cold or too warm. Whether she needed extra blankets or other comforts as she held her baby. A baby that, no matter how he looked at her, surely look like her dead husband.

Yes, a whole list of reasons not to go in. To protect her, her reputation, her privacy. To protect himself. For all the changes he'd begun to make about his past hadn't included her.

He heard her make a sound—something like a muffled sob—and he opened the door without a knock.

Too much. Too much emotion within her heart, in her head, in the very depths of her. Feelings roiling over her, burying her. Furrowing her heart, gouging through her soul.

It didn't matter what she did to occupy her time so that she might forget. Or at least have a momentary reprieve. She'd sleep all day, but her dreams were about Roger, Nicholas and the baby. She'd be awake, pacing the floor, requesting to read lost ledgers. None of it occupied her long enough for any true escape.

Bess would come to tell her the gossip, or talk about the general upkeep of Mei Solis. Rohesia would examine her, make sure she was healing from the birth. Both of them didn't have much else to say, or any valid reason for visiting her.

Bess had her own family obligations, and Matilda regretted it that her friend felt she had to visit her. The same for Rohesia, who had no real reason to see her about her health. She was healed from Julianna's birth. There were changes to her body, but as with other mothers they were permanent, and in that way, the markings and loosened skin was something she drew comfort from.

Still, Rohesia brought healing teas and tinctures. Acidic broth and choice cuts of meat. She knew the food and the drink would give her strength—the strength she needed to feed Julianna. She didn't know whether she'd ever feel strong again.

Sitting on the bed—the only piece of furniture in the room—Matilda clenched her fists. No tears. None. Only unending pain. It was worse when Bess took Julianna. Bess who had at first balked at taking the baby. Yet, Matilda didn't want her only seeing her mother like this.

All through Roger's burial and the months leading up to the birth, Matilda had held in her grief. She wanted her child only to know happiness. Not to feel the raw swinging of emotions, but to feel the calm assurance of her parents. It should have been Roger, too, but Julianna had only her.

She could barely hold any emotion in.

Worse, Julianna cried. And Matilda swore she did it because her mother couldn't. So she had begged Bess to take her out—just for a bit, just enough so her daughter would know the world didn't only encompass grief.

Even though her mother didn't believe it.

Grief. *Again.* She'd lost her mother a few years ago, and her father was slipping further away from her every day. She missed them both.

Yet, this…this *hurt.* Down to the very depths of her bones, which no longer seemed to want to hold her upright, so she spent her days around this bed, sleeping, sitting, pacing around it.

Today she'd had a different routine. Bess had brought in a bath and different clothes. Wanting, needing distraction, she'd accepted them. But she had found no comfort in the warmth of the water against her aching bones or her skin that felt so raw. No pleasure in the washing of her hair and the softness of the new clothes.

Now dried, and dressed in a loose chemise, she sat waiting for Bess to return and take the tub away, to bring back Julianna.

There were windows in her room, but she wasn't interested in the outside world. She didn't want to be reminded of the outside world.

'Is this how it's been?'

The deep voice, the familiar voice, whirled her around.

'Nicholas!'

She frantically wiped her face, aware acutely of her wet and unbound hair, her lack of a gown, the puffiness and redness of her cheeks.

'What are you doing here?'

He didn't look as if he would answer. His brow drew in and he had a tightness about his face. There was also a look of surprise and hesitancy, as if he didn't know how to answer, or didn't understand himself what had brought him here.

'I heard you, Matilda. I've been hearing you.'

She'd thought herself alone in her grief. Ridiculous. Of course the whole manor knew she was grieving. Rohesia and Bess were her constant reminders that she was holed up in this room. Their eyes checked her constantly for tears or moments of weakness.

She had been crying. Just these echoes of heaviness deep in her heart that forced themselves out of her. Those she couldn't stop. Most times she'd thought she had a hand to her mouth, or she'd bitten down on Julianna's blanket, or pressed her lips to Julianna's cheek.

Heard? She didn't even want to hear herself.

'Sorry.'

'That's not what I meant.'

Nicholas in her room…this room. Nicholas who had brought her here.

'Then what did you mean?'

He opened his mouth, closed it, and she knew that Nicholas was perhaps for the first time in his life uneasy.

He'd been Lord of Mei Solis since his father's death. Before that he'd been the privileged heir to a great estate. He'd trained until he became a warrior, a knight, a mercenary. Made himself formidable through his training, through his size, through his will. His sudden vulnerability stopped something inside her. She felt something unfurling.

'I wanted you to know I wasn't simply barging in here.'

'Even so, you did. Barge in here.'

She was only just now realising it. She should have realised it immediately, but the hesitancy in his manner had surprised her. She stood. A feeling other than grief was coming through to her. Discomfort. Frustration. Maybe embarrassment at having her privacy torn apart.

He'd brought her to this room. Given her this sanctuary. Did he think he had a right to watch her, see what she ate, hear the sounds that she wanted no one to hear, that *she* didn't want to hear?

'You didn't knock.'

'You've been here for three weeks.'

'You brought me here. I thought this was to be my room.'

'It is your room in which to rest, to find some peace, but not to hide.'

That hurt. She hadn't been hiding. It had been her sanctuary. And he was no innocent.

'Like you hid?'

'What is that supposed to mean?'

'You were injured years ago and you didn't come back.'

'I wasn't hiding. I was recovering.'

'And after that?' At his silence, she continued, 'Roger only died a few short months ago, Nicholas.'

'*He* died. Not you.'

She flinched and then rallied. 'What do you expect me to do? Go on with my days as if nothing had happened?'

'Death had happened, but so has life. And life requires more than death. It requires that you rest, that you eat. That you…' He pressed his lips together, shook his head. 'At the very least it requires food.'

He had been about to say that life required more than her sleeping and eating. But she knew life required more. She just didn't want to acknowledge that right now.

'They bring me food and water.'

'The trays are almost full when they are returned.'

She felt discomfort at his sudden presence. Ire at his accusation that she was hiding. Embarrassment at him watching her.

Then something stronger pierced through her grief.

Anger.

How *dared* he watch her, tell her she was hiding, that she wasn't eating enough? How dared he notice the sounds she made?

They were private. *Her* privacy. *Her* grief. *Her* feelings. He had no right to thoughts about them.

'Leave,' she said.

'Why do you send the food back, Matilda?'

'I eat enough to feed Julianna. This is my room. Leave me be.'

'Why are you staying in here? The window's closed. It's dark. The fire's barely lit.

'You brought me here—for what? To keep an eye on me? I trusted you.'

'You need to eat, Matilda.'

'I have no hunger. For anything.'

His eyes widened with shock at that. 'You need to eat, Matilda.'

'For what?'

'For *her*.'

'I'm doing that.'

His eyes searched the room as if for answers. 'For how long?'

'For as long as it takes.'

However, she didn't *know* how long, and she was already worried. Her milk was not flowing as she'd thought it would. She was eating enough for that, but her body wasn't co-operating. She was already worried that Bess had seen that and was having someone else feed Julianna. And that made her lie on the bed and stare at the ceiling, her body too tired to do anything else.

His eyes returned to hers. 'You need your strength for her.'

Anger. She'd needed to do a lot of things. Like be there when her husband was out in the fields. Taking care of his wound and agreeing to chop his foot off sooner. There were many dozens of things she hadn't done.

There must be something she hadn't done because he was gone. And she lived with the guilt of that, lived with more guilt than this man or anybody knew about.

She knew. What she didn't want was to hear it. Especially from him.

She marched over to him, waved her arms. 'Get out.'

He didn't move.

'Is this why you put me here. To trouble me and worry me? You're asking me questions you have no right to. As if—'

Suddenly cold, she grasped her arms around herself, turned around.

'Who do you think you are? *No one.* You left and we picked up after you. You left all in your glory to go and wave your sword and earn little metal pieces to buy things. We kept on farming when the wheat came, building when the walls were crumbling. You weren't out in the blustery gales tying down crops. Losing sheep in the culverts. When the west roof fell in on the manor and the rains came.'

Cold. Hot. Shaking. She hugged herself more. Her feet were taking her faster. She was aware that Nicholas stood as still as a wall. Doing what? Nothing? Listening to her raving? Being there for her?

He stood right there, right next to her, and still he was doing nothing.

'Get out!' She pushed against him.

He didn't move.

Frustrated, she pushed again and again, until something powerful nipped and pinched inside her. Rage.

With everything she had inside her, every bit

of strength she'd ever built, she shoved against his unyielding body and he took it. His breath as she jabbed at his abdomen was the only indication that he felt any of the storm breaking inside her.

She wanted to do more. Much more. And she glanced at his implacable expression and his formidable body and she knew he'd take more. More of whatever this was. He was *letting* her. He was doing nothing. Standing mute and still. He was letting her pour it all out. He was being *helpful*.

That knowledge spiked her anger. It was as if he had a right to this as well. Her room, her privacy, her thoughts. Now her emotions.

It overwhelmed her that she was doing this. Not sitting on the bed, trying to hold herself together, but falling apart. *Falling apart*.

The sounds she had held down inside her were coming out with her fists. Louder now that she didn't muffle them in the bedcovers. Grief, pain, agony released for anyone to see, to hear.

For this man to witness.

Until she shoved at him one more time, her

body slamming into his, and physically fell against him, panting hard. His arms came around hers, squeezing tight. Holding her in as she fell apart.

Matilda's sobs wrecked him in every possible way. It was her vulnerability, her broken heart, the way she pounded and shouted as if she was in a storm, lost at sea, and he was the hollow broken tree limb she clung to in order to keep afloat. He was all she had to keep her afloat.

Worthless—that was what he was. Broken. Hollow. The choked sounds she made were like a person taking in water. She was taking in feelings, and though she clung to him tightly, and he wrapped his arms around her with every bit of care and strength that he could give, it wasn't helping. She was still going under—and she was taking him with her.

And he let her.

He deserved it—*and* all the words she threw at him. Her hatred of him was clear in every bite of her accusation, every break between her denunciations. He *deserved* her pounding fists and battering palms. Smashing his walls, his stupidity. His pride.

For weeks she'd been like this, in the room next to his. Living with this fear and sorrow. And he'd *let* her. Married to another. No rights.

All true.

All false.

Because those things didn't matter—not after the promise he'd made to Rhain to return here and repair his past.

What kind of man was he that he hadn't given her a helping hand? Even if that hand was out of friendship? Broken as it was. Hollow, most likely. But there was substance there. There was their childhood.

For that sweet, innocent time he should have been standing by her all these days and nights. He should have taken her words and her fists, and let her repeat them every day. Let her cling to him when she was going under with her grief.

Instead, for almost three weeks he'd let her drown.

No more. He pulled her closer, lifted her so she didn't have to hold her own weight. When even that distance was too much he lowered his head and rested his cheek against her hair. After a moment she pulled her own head into the crook he'd made. As if being in that almost enclosed spot against his neck was the air she needed.

Bess knocked twice before she entered. Nicholas almost rose from the chair in the corner to stop her, but worried the weight of his boots would be amplified in the suddenly silent space.

Bess stopped and gaped. Her arms full of Julianna, her eyes went from him to Matilda, sleeping peacefully in the bed. And she looked peaceful, too, despite the tear tracks. There was a softness in her, as if something had lifted.

'She fell asleep,' he said.

Bess clutched the baby a bit closer.

'You can give her to me.' He held out his arms.

She took a couple of steps, stopped. 'What are you doing in here?'

'I merely had a conversation with her.'

'And stayed?'

'She needed rest.'

'And you stayed?' she repeated.

Matilda stirred and their gazes swung to hers.

'I knew you'd return soon,' he whispered. 'Hand the baby to me so she can rest, and then you can return to your home.'

Her eyes wary, Bess walked quietly to him and laid the babe in his arms.

Julianna did not stir, perfectly content, though it must have been hours since she'd been in the room.

'Has she fed?'

Bess hesitated.

'*Has* she?' he repeated though he knew the answer.

'There are many mothers available who are more than happy to help, knowing Matilda cannot.'

'Does she know?'

'We don't talk about it… I don't talk about it… But I think she knows because she gives me Julianna when she is wailing. Her milk may be going.'

Nicholas adjusted Julianna until she was held securely against him. He absorbed her sweet smell and gentle warmth. This child needed her mother, and her mother needed her.

'Is it the grief?'

'Rohesia thinks so.'

Matilda had been drowning in her emotions in the room right next to where he slept and her baby was going down with her. What good were his promises? Hollow. Worthless.

Not any more.

'I'll tend her.'

Bess fixed her gaze on Matilda, still sleeping. Then, with a glance he knew was a warning, she nodded and left the room.

A warning. It wouldn't be the first one he'd received, and soon he'd be receiving many more.

Fix his past.

When he'd left it had been only Mei Solis that had needed repairs. Now that he'd returned, his friendships, his relationships with these people, needed repair as well.

He had seen the peace Rhain had achieved. He'd thought he'd do anything to find that. Except he hadn't.

Temporary. No rights.

Even if his stay here *was* temporary, his relationships weren't. They'd continued even while he had ignored them for all these years. He hadn't said proper goodbyes.

He could never have time with Roger again, but if he could, what would he say? Only now could he allow himself such thoughts.

Louve wasn't the same as when he'd left. The casual ease was still there, but some fissure was running underneath his smiles. Was it because he'd stayed? Had he wanted to stay? A few more days, and many more drinks, and maybe the mystery that was there would be solved.

Mei Solis Manor itself had been managed to the utmost. A little more coin—which he had now brought—was all it needed to provide a good livelihood for the tenants. More sheep, more supplies for the blacksmith. All that.

He could fix his past.

But Matilda?

His heart?

Could he forgive her for marrying Roger? For not waiting for him? For thinking he'd lied when he'd said he loved her? How could she think so little of him? Think that he'd simply stopped writing and that was a rendering of their betrothal?

He'd done it to protect her, and yet no answer could she give him to make up for that letter he'd received while he'd lain there dying. Nothing.

His eyes fell to Julianna. But for his friendship with Roger, for his friendship with Matilda in the past and for this baby here, he would make it easier for them. He might be injured, his body scarred as well as his soul. He might be hollow and worthless. However, if she would cling to him a little longer he'd make certain that she and Julianna didn't drown, but made it to the shore before he left.

He pulled the blanket more securely around Julianna. The baby slept, the mother slept, and for the first time since he'd returned Nicholas's restlessness was still as well.

Chapter Eleven

February 1296

Mere months and Matilda's life had completely changed. She sat at her own table in her own home and held her child as she fed. Julianna, her daughter, was more beautiful than she could ever have imagined. From her toes to her fingers, from the darkness of her hair and the stubbornness of her chin, so like her father's. And Julianna was a *girl*—something she'd known all along.

This was the life she wanted. A home. A hearth. Good friends…family. She wanted to hold on to it so desperately.

Julianna was her life now—a tiny baby, completely dependent on her—and she knew she was already using her as a shield against life's greatest agony. Death. Loss. Roger had done that. Defended her. Julianna would never know that.

Matilda gasped. *So much loss.* Julianna would never know her father—the way he'd smiled, the ease of his kind words. And his patience. Her daughter would never know of his patience.

She rubbed her daughter's hair, which already looked darker than her own. Roger's hair. Maybe Roger's eyes. Definitely his nose.

'He knew her.'

Her hand still on Julianna's head, Matilda whirled around. Nicholas was there, holding her gaze but looking unsure. A strange look for a man who made his life killing.

Death should have become familiar to him. Yet she could see from the lines of his face, the line of his shoulders, that he carried a great weight. It was in the hesitancy of his step and the cadence of his words. His words which somehow were all too sure. and he continued them.

'It's what you were thinking, about the babe?' he continued. 'Tiny, fragile, new. She didn't have enough time to know him. He knew *her*, though.

Before he died he already loved his child, even if she wasn't yet born. I envy him that.'

'Well, there's nothing to envy now.' A daughter with no father. *Like her.*

He looked at Julianna, his eye softening. 'There's *everything* to envy.'

'Pity, you mean. A woman with no husband… a child with no father. And no land of our own except what he did for you. Do you think my labours will be enough?'

'Can I take her? There's food, and I know you haven't eaten.'

She clenched Julianna tighter to her. 'She's not crying. I'd rather not disturb her yet.'

He nodded. 'I'll get the food, then.'

'And do what? Feed me?'

'If need be.'

'To make certain I don't weaken and you lose coin?'

'We're past that now, aren't we?'

He moved to the fireplace—she presumed to put on another log, to make it warmer. Instead he threw a bucket of water on it and turned back to face Matilda.

'You can't stay here on your own. You'll stay at the manor through the rest of winter. It's too cold for Julianna to be in a cottage.'

Matilda's eyes broke from her trance. The relieved look in her gaze told him he'd said the right thing.

Neither of them said a word on the path to the manor. As if his words had made sense in the chaos that was their life.

It was the cold. Of course it was the cold that drove her from her home. The cruelty of winter and the storms that battered against the feeble boards and windows had mocked the little fireplace inside. It was only that, and not the fact that her husband, father to her child and lifetime friend, was dead.

He held out his arms. 'Give her to me.'

She gave a tiny shake of her head and clutched Julianna closer.

Fear. Pain. She still needed reassurances. Those he could give to his mercenaries, but what did he tell this woman he'd once loved, whom he still loved, when she'd lost the man she'd chosen over him? Reassurances of what?

Then he knew. 'I have held her before,' Nicholas said. 'On the day she was baptised. I didn't drop her then.'

Gasping at that, she let her eyes, which had lost their focus, gaze on him. He wanted to comfort her when he had not the right. Nonetheless, she had loosened her hold, and he could take advantage of it. Carefully extracting the baby from her arms, he nestled her against him.

'Why did you do it?' she asked. Her voice was hoarse with unshed tears.

He looked over his shoulder and saw a woman grieving. He grieved with her. No matter what had happened between them, he grieved for her loss and his own.

'Why did *you* carry the baby to the church that day and not Bess or Rohesia? Why did you agree to be her godparent?'

'The Lord of the Manor is usually asked to be godparent.'

However, that didn't explain why Bess or Rohesia hadn't carried the baby, though it was customary for a woman to carry the baby if she was a girl. But explanations and reasons weren't what

Matilda was asking him for. So he told her the truth.

'I carried her because you needed me to. And you've needed me before, haven't you, Matilda? But I wasn't here. And so you found Roger. And now you've lost Roger, and nothing I can do or say will make up for that. I'm so sorry, Matilda.'

They walked on in silence for a while longer, Nicholas nestling Julianna tightly in his arms.

'I'm sorry for that day,' he said.

Deep in her thoughts, she wondered if she'd lost track of what he was saying. 'What day?'

'It wasn't your fault I received that letter then. You'd sent it a month before, but we were travelling and it took time to reach me. I received it the same day I received my injury.'

It had arrived when he was at death's door. The worst day of his life somehow made worse.

'Did it give you strength, my letter? Did your hatred for me help you?'

He wouldn't lie to her. 'Yes.'

That hurt, but it was better than the alternative. Something that had hurt him so much he hadn't wanted to get out of bed.

'Sorry,' he said again.

She tried to tease him. 'I've never known you to apologise so much before.'

'I have a lot to apologise for.'

So did she. Still.

'And is this because of Roger? You feel I'm owed these apologies now because I'm a widow?'

'Matilda, just let a man do what he needs to.'

'So you can have a clear conscience because your friend is dead?'

'I was wrong to blame you!' he growled. 'It wasn't your fault you fell in love with him. I can see why it happened now. And it wasn't wrong of you to write to me and tell me about it.'

'I'm very glad your hatred for me fuelled your recovery!'

'You are the most impossible female I have ever known!'

'In all those grand countries and exciting adventures? I doubt it.'

'There's nothing grand about that life, I can assure you, Matilda.'

'So is that why you returned home?' Matilda asked.

'Rhain told me to.'

She raised her eyebrows at him. 'You take orders from other people?'

'He didn't exactly tell me to return here, but he wanted me to face my past.'

Nicholas's past wasn't Mei Solis. It might have been significant for his father, but for him the manor had only ever been stone and mortar... and something he didn't want. There were no other ghosts here for him to face...except her.

He had returned to face *her*. All this time she'd felt him watching and waiting. Would he confront her now?

'Why did he think you needed to fix the past?'

'Are you asking how he knew me so well?'

She shook her head. 'You mentioned him in some of your letters.'

'The ones I did write to you.' Nicholas looked over her shoulder. 'I had almost forgotten those.'

She hadn't. Those letters, received almost every new moon, were all she'd had of him those first years he was away. When she'd married Roger she'd wrapped the letters and placed them in the bottom of her chest. She should have seen her actions for what they were—known that part of her had never stopped loving Nicholas.

'How could you forget them?'

His gaze returned to her. 'I didn't forget my feelings for you. They were all I had left. No family. No home. Just you and the times we'd shared, the feelings we'd shared.'

'Yet you stopped writing to me?'

'Yes.'

Just like that she felt the cracks in her heart open again. There was a part of her that still believed if she had stopped loving this man and given herself to Roger completely then he wouldn't have been out in the fields at every moment. Maybe a truer love would have completed him—completed *her.* They wouldn't have sought their happiness elsewhere.

Elsewhere? There was nowhere else for her. Mei Solis was her home. And, though she argued otherwise, though he did as well, Mei Solis belonged to Nicholas.

'Why did you come back? When you say you wanted to face your past, you mean face me. Did you come back to face me?'

His face turned implacable, as if he was holding a terrible secret. It made her angry. Roger was dead, her mother was dead, and she only had her father part of the time.

'Why didn't you wait for me?' he demanded. 'I was out there risking my life for coin to provide for you. To build you a—'

'Oh, don't say it. Are you comparing me to Helena? When have I *ever* cared for wealth or belongings?'

He had tried to pretend she had, but he knew it wasn't that. 'You were selfish—just like her. Taking your pleasures where you could.'

If he had struck her she wouldn't have been more surprised. 'I have *never* been selfish.'

'You married behind my back.'

'You broke my trust!' she said. 'You left after I begged you not to. Sent a letter almost every new moon, and then suddenly you stopped writing!' She waved her arms, turned away from him. 'You've given me reasons for this, but we both know you could have put *something* in the missives you sent to Louve. Yet, you didn't. Just… nothing.'

She stabbed a finger above her heart.

'And you dare compare me to Helena? Me, who stayed and helped care for every one of the tenants you abandoned. Who cares for her father, and Agnes, and at least—'

She broke then—just broke. It was more than her trust. He'd broken her pride. Her begging him not to leave had been in front of everyone. The looks of pity had lasted for years afterwards.

But she couldn't say that to him. What little pride she had left refused to yield to him. But she was vulnerable, and Nicholas knew it, because he held out his hand as if to help her.

'Don't!' she warned him, changing what she wanted to say to what she needed to. 'Don't make this about me. It was you, with your promises as empty as your father's. Telling me you'd stay, but leaving within the year. Telling me you'd return, but year after year you didn't. Telling me you'd write, and then the letters stopped. You broke something in me with your actions. How could I ever trust you again?'

Nicholas soothed Julianna, who had stirred in his arms, no doubt disturbed by the angry voices over her head. He lowered his voice, desperately trying to rein in the emotion behind the words he spoke.

'Every action I took was to uphold my promise to you. To give you a home, a family, a life here. We couldn't have that if I didn't earn the coin. I was faithful to you all those years. Though we spent many nights in inns full of women. Though I travelled to foreign lands and their customs were different when it came to marriage. It took me years to return, but I told you I would earn coin and come back to you, and I did.'

He exhaled, rubbed the back of his neck with one hand while he held the baby in the crook of his arm.

'It's true my father never kept promises, and so I never learned trust. Not from my father nor from a stepmother, who broke her trust the moment she clapped eyes on this heap of land. I trusted *you*. I gave you my heart, my everything, but you didn't believe me. And, try as I might, I don't understand.'

She turned from the anguish in his gaze. It was three years since she'd sent that letter telling him she was marrying another. How to explain what had happened to her at that time?

Weak. Vulnerable. Everything in her became small as she listened to his words. But if she told him all her vulnerabilities then she'd only be weaker. That little bit of pride she had left would be gone.

He'd taken everything else—she wouldn't give him this. So she remained turned away from him and she also remained silent.

Nicholas exhaled roughly. A sound of angry frustration. 'I depended on you, Matilda. Everything that was worth anything was with you.'

She heard him pacing away, his words getting louder.

'My heart. My soul. I bet everything on your trust. You who had had it all your life. Who knew what it was and how strong it could be. I bet my *life* on your trust. And where did it go?'

'I remained faithful to you as well. All those years I wrote to you, and I prized those letters you sent me. I was surprised when my letters didn't come, but Louve's did. Then another one was missing, and another. Then my mother died…and my father didn't fare well. *I* didn't fare well.

Nicholas made some rough sound. He was breaking now—just like her. She knew why, too, because every word was the truth.

He hadn't been wrong to put his trust in her. But she had been weak. She hadn't trusted herself. If she had, she would have realised that Nicholas must have a reason for not writing. All she'd had to do was trust that. Trust him.

Instead, she'd let her pride get in the way. It was true that she'd never been tested like that before—never been pushed to those limits, with his support gone, her mother's death, her father's deterioration. But those were just excuses, really, because at the first hurdle she had fallen. Embarrassed, shamed, she had wrapped herself in pride and hadn't let anyone close enough to see the weakness she was hiding.

A mistake—and she had hurt so many people. Roger. Nicholas. Her father. Herself.

She'd been hurting *herself.* That was why she'd wanted to change who she was. Not because

Nicholas had left, but because she hadn't wanted to be reminded of who she was.

She marched ahead. However, she knew Nicholas's gaze was still on her. So much pain between them. So many mistakes to remedy. And not all were in the past. More words needed to be said. Those she'd tried to speak earlier. Those needed to be said.

'I cared for Roger the best I could,' she said. 'I stayed. I cared. But it wasn't enough. Nothing I did or continue to do, nothing I was or continue to be is enough!'

Without another word, she took her daughter from him arms and walked away from Nicholas, towards the only regret she could remedy.

Chapter Twelve

How much time did he have? Nicholas swung the horse outside the gate. None. He had none. Matilda hadn't been seen since she'd returned to the manor. Bess had reported that Matilda had fed Julianna and then left for a walk.

Why had he let her go?

He'd known when she'd stalked off with Julianna in her arms that matters weren't settled between them. But he'd thought to give her more time. In the meantime, Matilda had managed to enter the stables, saddle one of the mares and ride off.

It had been hours since they'd talked. Hours during which he'd let her alone—because her voice had sounded so lost, her words had gutted him, because he hadn't known what he wanted to say.

He couldn't push his horse to gallop any faster. Not for the first time he cursed his size, his weight, the fact he had only one eye. Fighting, walking, he'd conquered it all—but not this. Not navigating a horse which was sensitive to his every shift. And at a horse's speed his peripheral vision was limited. He could be rushing past her.

He cursed the loss of his eye all over again as he sped across terrain that was no longer familiar. Yet, somehow he knew that she would ride over the fields through the sparse copse of trees towards the woods. That was familiar, and yet it had been years since he'd ridden this way.

In their youth, they'd ridden recklessly out this way, towards the low shrubbery and the low stone walls that dotted this area of his land. Part open field, part obstructed. Only the most skilled horseman could manoeuvre a horse through such territory. In their youth they'd often raced and jumped through the open field.

Now the shrubbery wasn't so low, and the grass was taller. The stone walls were partially obscured. And there she was! Her horse ran at a slower pace than his, but he felt no relief. She was raising herself in the saddle, bending her body low.

Did she intend to jump? Matilda had told him she hadn't ridden in years. Her body had changed and so had the terrain. It was too dangerous.

'Matilda!' he shouted.

Startled, she pulled sharply to the left on her reins as she looked over her shoulder. The horse skidded to the side, but she got it under control again and urged it forward. Faster this time.

Matilda heard nothing of Nicholas behind her. Nothing but the harsh breath of her horse, her own shortened breath as the jarring of its hooves crushed the grass. The field was uneven, and she dodged around shrubbery and holes.

She didn't want Nicholas behind her, cornering her at the taller hedges they'd used to jump. Maybe at this speed she could make it. It had been so long. Why had she stopped riding?

Movement to her right—the head of Nicholas's horse. Too close.

Her heart beating faster, she leaned down, preparing for the jump. His horse gained on her, pushing her to the side. Her mount started to slow and she pressed her knees in tighter. But Nicholas forced the turn.

There would be no jumping, but she refused to stop. Snapping the reins, she let out a shout and her mount burst forth again. Nicholas made a similar sound, but she was ahead this time, and turned towards the woods. Her smaller mount would make it through the trees. His horse would not.

A whistle, loud and shrill, shot across her, and her horse immediately responded. No words, no snapping of the reins changed matters. The horse knew a command and listened. It skittered under her while she continued to force it forward. Another whistle and it yanked its head out of her control and stopped.

Matilda gripped her saddle while Nicholas tossed his reins and dismounted. His expression was dark and menacing, emblazoned with exertion and rage. The whiteness of his scar was like a lightning slash across his face.

Coursing under her skin she felt the exhilaration of the ride and the chase, the certainty she had been about to fall. Her horse was too small for that jump. Nicholas had known it—she had not.

Still she refused to dismount, but his height was to his advantage and his strong hands hauled her off and away.

When he set her on the ground he looked as if he wanted to put her back on the horse so she could ride to her death. Even so, for the first time in so long she felt *alive*.

'Why did you do it?' he bit out. 'Why did you risk it? That horse is too small to make that jump. And riding like that—one mud puddle could have killed you!'

Her legs were unsteady, but some unknown strength held her up. 'I was riding my horse.'

He pointed his hand towards her. 'You've never ridden like that! Was the saddle secure? You were sliding sideways.'

She swiped his accusing hand away. 'It wasn't the saddle. It was the terrain. You think you weren't leaning as much as me? I was at full strength—you forcing my horse to the side could have got them tangled. Both of us killed.'

'I forced that turn to get to you. To my surprise, you then headed to the woods.'

'You have no responsibility for me. You left.'

She didn't need this. Shouldn't *want* this. Not now, when everything broken within her had almost righted itself.

She'd nearly fallen. Had been certain she would when her horse had started shying away from the jump she had committed to before Nicholas had forced the change in direction.

However, until that moment—*during* that moment when she had been about to catapult over— everything in her had become whole again.

She hadn't felt like herself in six years. The years of Nicholas's absence, her marriage to Roger, her trying to be like him. Her mother's death, her father's deterioration. Roger's death.

Riding with no care, she had felt free, and it had been glorious. She'd be damned if this glowering man ruined it.

Spinning around, she marched to her horse.

He leapt to her side. 'Now you ignore me?'

Her horse shied as she approached, which only angered her more. 'I was ignoring you before. *You* were the one who came after me!'

'If I hadn't, where would you be? Dead! That horse is lame.'

'The horse is fine. Move away so I can get to her.'

'It's skittering away because it has more sense than you.'

'You are being ridiculous. Just go. I'm alive. The horse isn't lame. You can go back to your home now. Whack around your sword with Louve.'

'Not when you almost caused your own death.' Nicholas stepped back, ran a hand through his hair. 'Did you *want* to die?

She whirled around. 'Of course I didn't want to die! Is that what you thought?'

She relished Nicholas stepping back. It was her turn to be the wild beast. She was free, and whatever was inside her could roam.

'When you first left, I rode, but no one rode with me. Your absence weighed heavy inside me and I stopped jumping. I stopped giving the horses rein to run, to be free. I was incapable of feeling any such lightness and I forced them to temper theirs.'

At first, there had been a part of her that had blamed herself, but after six years she had known the blame lay with him.

'You left because of your own restlessness.'

'I left because the manor—'

'No! You will admit it. There was something inside you that thrilled at leaving Mei Solis behind.'

He exhaled roughly. 'Then my leaving was my choice.'

A victory—but not enough. He wouldn't get away with it this time. '*Why* were you restless, Nicholas? Why? Because there wasn't anything here for you? Because what you needed wasn't here?'

'I loved you.'

'Not enough.'

When she'd been flying across the field, the wind had whipped at her hair so it had stung her eyes. She had been flying, and his words had pulled at her and crashed her to the ground.

'I wasn't enough. So I remade myself. I stopped riding. Took care of my father and taught Agnes how to draw. I spent time with Roger.'

She clenched her eyes at the piercing memory.

'He had peace inside him. He always knew his place in the world. This place was enough. And the more time we spent together the more he made me believe that I was enough...for him. Even as broken as I was, he wanted me. You left, and I was less than I was. I *had* less of myself— less of a heart. But...but my being less was what he wanted. How could I not want him, too?'

'Matilda—

She raised her hand against his words, against what he wanted to say. She wanted to hold off his apologies, his sorrow. She heard both in just his saying her name.

'There's more. Let me tell you more.'

Maybe it was her words, or more likely the emotion she'd sunk into those words, but this giant of a man stood still to listen to her. The sun's fading light played across the darkness of his hair, over the impenetrable light at the back of his gaze.

He wanted something from her. And she'd no longer avoid it. He had returned to Mei Solis wanting something from her. She'd been waiting.

Yet he'd held his frustration. Watched her... waited. She'd dined with him in the Great Hall, they'd made decisions during council meetings, he had held her hand when she gave birth to her daughter. All these months he'd stayed by her side.

And she'd started to fall in love with him again.

This time it hadn't been easy at all. This time it hurt. And still Nicholas had watched and waited. He wanted something from her, and right now she would give it to him.

'I loved Roger as a friend, and as a husband. It was easy to come home to him. He made it easy.'

'Are you telling me everything we did together was *hard*?'

Everything in her life had been easy. The love of her family...falling in love with Nicholas. And then it hadn't been easy any more. His father had worked, and Helena had come. Nicholas had accepted the challenge his life had become. He'd challenged her. He was challenging her now. Nothing had been hard between them until the day he'd left. Then every day had been a challenge.

He was demanding an answer now. She'd give him more than that. So much more. A dizzying giddiness overtook her. Like hysteria with an edge.

'You want a confession, Nicholas?' she mocked. 'Is that why you chased me? Is that why you've been doggedly following me? Taking care of me, of Julianna, while Roger grows colder in his grave?'

His demeanour turned icy. He didn't like that at all, and she fought the urge to laugh again.

'I didn't take care of you or Julianna to get a confession!' he said. 'I did it because I care for you!'

'Care? I'm a woman full-grown. Do you think I can't feel need and desire when it's so close to me? You think I can't recognise yours? It brushes against my skin and it takes my breath away. It always did. Your desire…mine. I recognise that all too well.'

'I want to care for you. You need that care.'

'You've shown that to me. Which makes this much easier to say. And you need to know the truth. It's what you've been wanting from me.'

'I don't need words. You don't have to tell me anything. This is enough.'

He didn't have the right to make that choice. Only she knew what was enough. She'd lived with barely enough for years. Now 'enough' would mean *everything*.

'I didn't love Roger as a lover should. I never did.'

'No…' he whispered. 'Don't.'

She wanted to laugh as the sudden weight of the truth lifted from her chest.

'You must hear the awful truth of it. Every time he held me I compared him to you. We barely kissed, barely held hands. But when you held me I was home and yet flying to far-off lands. There was a promise in your kisses. Of more…so much more.'

He closed his eye, as if the memory of those times pierced him as well.

'There was no *more* with Roger,' she whispered. 'You want to know why we didn't have a baby earlier? I'll tell you truth. Because we were more friends than lovers. I shared his bed, but it wasn't always a marriage bed. When the need got too great—and it did—he was there. And he was there when he asked me to marry him. Defending me, shielding me, protecting me. I knew I wasn't enough for him. That a piece of my heart would never be his and that he couldn't have all my body either. And even though I wasn't all his, he still asked me.'

Nicholas didn't look relieved by her words. He didn't look anything except tortured. As if her words had taken the weight off her chest and dropped it on his. Why? Shouldn't he be happy that Roger's touch had been kind, but had never filled her with desire? But he looked as if he couldn't stand it. Was his pain for her or for his dead friend?

'The horses,' he finally said. 'You drew them everywhere.'

Was he avoiding the subject? Or perhaps finding another way of saying it? Because she knew what he meant. The horses were part of this confession too.

'You guessed the truth. I realised it before I saddled that horse. Something in me was trying to get free again. So I let it. And then you...' She exhaled, letting the pressure that was building up inside her be released. 'You can't stop me. No one can. And I won't let it happen again.'

It was the truth. Swearing on her very soul, she meant it. She intended to be there for her father, her daughter, for her home. But she wouldn't give herself away again. And that meant not to this man.

Matilda was standing like a light in the coming darkness. Her red-gold hair fluttered in the breeze, highlighted by the green trees behind her. The woods were tranquil—he was not.

Nicholas's entire body still shuddered from wresting her from that horse. He'd had no saddle. Nothing to anchor him except the depth of his training and his strength.

Right now he had no more strength. He'd

thought she wanted to die, but she was telling him she wanted to live. Everything inside him exalted in that truth.

'I don't want to stop you. I don't want to rein you in.'

She blinked. 'What is it that you *do* want, Nicholas? I've told you everything now.'

No, she hadn't. There had been no words of love or marriage or a future together. Even so, he wanted those. God, he wanted those. His heart thumped in his chest with the absolute need for it.

But he had to stop himself from grabbing her. Because there were words that needed to be said. Thank goodness they were simple words.

'I want you.'

She shook her head and a frown began. 'Didn't you listen?'

He wasn't saying it right. What could he say to make her believe? 'I don't want the woman you were. I want the woman you've become.'

'Not a word. You have understood not a word of what I said.'

He reached out, grabbed her arm. His hold was

gentle when truly he wanted to crush her to him. 'Don't ignore me or run away this time.'

She pulled free and he let her, but that was all he'd give her after what she'd told him.

'You don't have that privilege now. I did hear you, and now you must listen to me—though I'll fumble the words.'

'I don't want to hear them.'

He scoffed. 'You were *begging* to hear them.'

'When have I ever begged?'

He pointed to the horses. 'When you mounted that horse and risked your life. When you explained what you did. So you *will* listen to me and you *will* hear me this time.'

He took a moment, thought hard. This moment was important. She needed to understand matters he couldn't fully grasp himself. Not after everything had been one way and now was another.

'I want you. Now. So much more than before. You feel guilty because you didn't love Roger enough, but you did love him. You lived—and I did, too. Whatever this is between us now, it's because of our years apart. It's because you married Roger and had Julianna. It's because you longed for horses and carved them in stone. It's because you found sensibility, and yet there's mischief in you all the same.'

She shook her head.

'I don't want to rein you in, and I don't want you as you were, but as you are *now*. That desire has only grown in my being in your company these last months.'

'I have told you I gave only part of myself to another man.'

'You told me you don't need a man to make you whole.' He gestured to the horses, now calmly eating. 'You found it with them. With whatever you let loose that was locked inside you.'

Her eyes... Those hazel eyes were surprised. It was better than the look she'd had before. Defiance. Hurt...

'I have been listening.' He walked to her horse, but he was in no hurry to return home. There were more words to be said first—some understanding between them that he needed...that *they* needed.

'Just because you don't need me it doesn't mean you don't want me.'

He could only see her profile now, and he felt that loss, but he knew it would give her time to come to an understanding of what he was telling her.

'You said the desire between us brushes against your skin. Know that what I feel for *you* isn't so light as a brush. It's like claws against my insides. Hot. Insistent. Relentless.'

'Even now?'

He looked over his shoulder. 'Do you doubt it?'

Her lips parted. He recognised that it wasn't in surprise this time, but because she needed to catch her breath.

'You want me though I have stretch marks and my belly will no longer be flat, though my nipples may never recover.'

Maybe the physical changes they'd both experienced were easier to talk about than the emotional. Even so, he still needed to say more words. Now, and quickly. His need for her would soon overwhelm any reasoning.

Matilda had confessed she wanted him. *Still*. He wanted to roar.

Words, he cautioned himself. *Just a few more.*

'You being a mother...' He took a breath,

steadying himself even as his body tightened in readiness for her. 'I've never seen a more beautiful thing in my life.'

'And the fact that the baby is Roger's?'

'Seeing you together…it *fills* me somehow. The fact that I know she's Roger's means I overflow with emotions I can't express. I was never good with words, and now I wish had the ability to tell you. Roger and I were in all true sense of the word brothers. I can't blame you for falling in love with him. He was always easy like that. And it was wrong of me to think you should stay alone when I… I wasn't here. When…' He swallowed hard, but Matilda needed to know this truth as well. 'When I also wasn't alone. I was faithful at first, I promise you. But after I received the letter, and this eye had healed enough, there were women I shared a bed with.'

She made some sound he couldn't interpret. 'I wouldn't expect you to be alone. You shouldn't have been alone.'

He hadn't been alone, but he had still been lonely. 'None of them were you.'

'I was married.'

'*You* were happy.'

He could see them together. Roger quiet, Matilda assertive. Their marriage would have been good. But he couldn't think of Roger kissing her, holding her. He couldn't think of Matilda's responses, Because despite what he felt about both of them, despite Matilda's confession about their marriage, jealousy was still there. He envied their time together, but he could still see their happiness.

'What is all this, Nicholas?' she asked. 'What are you telling me?'

'I didn't wish for his death. I had made peace with your being with him. I want you to understand that before—' He needed to say this right. 'I have a truth to tell as well, Matilda. I can't be sorry. I can't be completely filled with grief because a great man—a better man than I—is dead. I *can't.*'

'Why?' she said.

And suddenly it became easier, because the words were simple. 'Because I love you.'

Chapter Thirteen

Matilda turned away from his words, from the look in his gaze. The one that could see her very soul if she let it.

He loved her.

Her heart leaped at the words, but they weren't right. They couldn't be…

'What did you say?'

'You heard me.'

Nicholas's voice was almost touching her—an indication of how close he had stepped. His hands suddenly rested on her shoulders, his long fingers lightly clenching them in their grip. His body was so much larger than hers, so much more lethal than hers. Immense. Formidable. Powerful. Nicholas was at her back. His legs were directly behind hers, along with the heat of him, the strength of him, the resistance of him.

What *was* this? A moment in time?

She looked away. 'Even after…?'

'Even after, before and for ever. I tried not to. I wanted to hate you. Your letter hurt me more than my physical wounds. However, no deed or word could kill my love for you. *Nothing.* I returned here hoping that merely seeing you with Roger would make it the truth for me. Allow the stubborn part of my heart to truly let go of the past.'

'But Roger wasn't here.'

'He wasn't. And at first I thought that would change everything. That my anger towards you both would fall on you.'

What had held him back? 'Perhaps you couldn't be angry with a woman carrying a child.'

'I couldn't be angry with *you* carrying a child without a husband by your side. I couldn't stop loving everything about you…'

She couldn't see him, but felt he spoke the truth. It was there in the steady emphasis of each word so she could hear him. It was there in the unsteadiness of his breath, as if his heart beat too fast.

She couldn't take this. It was too much. All her feelings were pouring out of her all too suddenly, after the recklessness of the horse ride, the fear as she'd realised she wouldn't make the jump, his turning the horse in another direction.

She felt as if he was turning *her* in another direction. That incredulous moment when he'd pulled her off the saddle, wrapped her in his arms and held her. She was held by him now. Secure. And yet vaulting through her was every feeling she'd ever had with him. Joy. Pride. Longing. Anguish. Resolve.

And now she had this new emotion: a realisation that both stung and freed her. Their separation had never been about him, but her. She had broken her own heart.

'I didn't know I loved you, but I should have.'

He kept his hands on her shoulders but he didn't turn her, and she didn't turn around either. It was as if whatever words they needed to say to each other needed to be felt in their touch as well as in their sounds.

'Don't apologise.'

'You must have hated me.'

'I hated you when I received that letter. And I hated you all the years since. But all that's changed.'

'I don't understand.'

She tried to turn, but his right hand slipped across her collarbone to her other shoulder as his left hand trailed down to her waist. He swamped her with his body, blanketed her with comfort. He didn't want to face her now, but whatever he wanted to say he needed her to hear it, and he pulled her against him, to ensure she heard every word.

'It wasn't right for me,' he said. 'However, it was right for *you*. How could I doubt it was right for you? Seeing you happy. Seeing Julianna being born. It was right for you, and I'm grateful you did it.'

That was why he held her like this. When his words sank in and she lost the strength in her legs he held her so he could pull her closer.

'I wouldn't have done it had I known,' she whispered.

His head bowed. His cheek rested against hers. She felt his breath against her neck. Felt his words vibrate against her back and inside her heart.

'I'm grateful you did it,' he repeated, his arms gently squeezing her tighter. 'Do you understand me? For you, for him. For the baby.'

She didn't understand. Couldn't. It was too much of a turnaround. She'd fled on that horse to escape one truth, only to realise her understanding was a lie. This was the truth.

'Because you love me,' she said.

'Because you deserve it. All of you deserved it. My loving you is something…*more*.'

Not enough support. Her hand went to his wrist, resting on her collarbone. Her arm wrapped around him. Back to front. Drawn into him as tightly as she could. The movement lifted her up until she fitted against him perfectly.

A quick change to his breath, but it soon evened out again. Her own breath was not quite there. He loved her. Showed her in all the ways that counted. Her breath was not evening out at all. It was becoming deeper under the weight of his arm. Against the heat of his body.

Say it.

Though the danger of what would happen shook through her body, the enormity of his confession pounded through her very soul.

Say it.

But something held her back from confessing that she loved him, too.

It would be too easy to say it—as if the words had always been there, beating under the surface. Those words to Nicholas *shouldn't* be easy. Her love for him should have been gone after she'd married Roger.

Guilt held her back. Shame for not loving her husband enough. Yet there was joy, too, because she believed every word Nicholas had said. It was the way he held her. This new tension between them that clutched him tightly to her. It needed no words.

Need. Want. Desire. This time not a confession of the heart but of the body. That was there. That had never gone away. She'd always wanted him.

As much as she'd loved her husband, whatever

had been between her and Nicholas had never died. His touch, his look, the way he smelled and felt. But never had they gone too far. Always waited. But their need for each other... That she'd remembered over the years. That she had never forgotten even as another man claimed her.

Even pregnant, she'd been acutely aware of Nicholas's return. His sitting next to her for hours as they held council. How close he was.

She couldn't speak the words, but with her body she'd tell him. Using his arm around her waist and his wrist on her collarbone, she pulled herself up until they fitted once more.

His breath hitched. There was a loosening of his arms as if he meant to step away. She gripped his hand and arm and kept him locked to her.

'Matilda...' he rasped.

'You love me?' she said.

'Yes.'

'Then love me.'

A choked growl. 'Do you know what you're asking of me? Of *us*?'

'I want it. I want you. I've always wanted you.'

His hands flexed on her. Just this side of clenching her tightly to him.

'It's been too long.'

She didn't want to think of the others he'd held like this.

He lowered his head once again. His lips pressed against her collarbone. Her neck.

'Too long since I held you. Kissed you.'

Not others. *Her.* He was thinking of her.

'There's no going back after this, Matilda.'

They weren't young any more. Both had learned about life and consequences. Holding him like this would have consequences.

She might not be able to tell him, but she didn't want to go back. The past held nothing for her any more.

'I know.'

Nicholas's body shuddered at her words. She'd had a man and knew what to expect. Except this was Nicholas. This was different.

She knew it was different in the way he held still behind her. Waiting for something from her. Waiting... But in that waiting were myriad needs.

There were prickles to the small of her back, a sudden sheen to her skin. Her hands were damp, sliding against him. Their breath changed to a matching rhythm. As if something reckless and dangerous was coming.

This was dangerous. For even though it was Nicholas, even though she'd wanted him all these years and he'd returned, she wasn't certain he'd stay.

Everything about him was a warrior, a mercenary. It was there in his restlessness. It was there in the way his body was made. There was no waste to any of him. Every bone, sinew, muscle and strength was on display, necessary to carry out a threat or offer protection.

He'd trained in all those years away, and he'd trained upon his return. Nicholas was a hired sword, and even now it was apparent. It was there in the predatory manner he held, as if waiting to strike. Lethal. Deadly.

Hers.

She wanted all that power, that strength, that resolve.

'Please…'

Desire coiled tight until she thought she'd break. Again she moved to turn around. Again he held her still against the hard rigidness of his stance. She felt the flexing tension of the muscles in his arms around her.

'Wait,' he said.

'No, I—'

'Like this,' he said, releasing his upper hold on her. He kept his left hand hard on her hip. Using his hand, his fingers, his palm to hold her still, he skimmed along her collarbone, up to her neck. Tilted her head with a caress of his thumb on her jaw.

She felt its rough callous against the tender skin under her ear, the heated gentleness of his hand cradling her before he brushed his knuckles along her cheekbone. Then down her neck. He brushed her hair away from her nape. Lowering his head that bit more, curling his fingers under her chin to bare her neck and skim his lips along her left ear.

The heat from his breath as his tongue traced coiled delicate curves was gentle. Devastating. While his breath grew ragged warm pleasure seeped into her belly, between her legs, and she leaned into his firm hand at her hip, the secure stance of his body.

Wanting more, she tried to turn.

His grip tightened. 'No.'

'I want to see you.'

There was a slight lessening of his hold, enough to give her permission. She took it.

His gaze was taking in every bit of her face, as if he hadn't seen her for most of his life. She knew she looked at him just the same way. Her gaze felt greedy.

'I want to *see* you,' she repeated.

There was a slight tremble to his hand and he closed his eye. Then he lowered his head even more, held still, and she reached behind him to untie the strip of linen covering his left eye.

Before she lowered it she took in all his features. The crease between his brows, the tightness around his jaw. It was as if what she did pained him. Yet she also saw the trusting way he waited, the softness of his lips.

She brushed her lips against his. Enough to taste him. To reward him for giving her this. He took a trembling breath, as if she had truly gentled him. Then she pulled the linen away.

Holding it in her left hand, and resting her other against his chest, she took in the full breadth of his injury.

He let her. Keeping his good eye closed. Allowing her to take in the scar without feeling the scrutiny of his gaze. Making the left and the right side of his face match though they never really could.

The scar was thin, healed as evenly as any scar could ever be. The scar was thin, but it bisected his brow, crossed his eyelid and ran down his cheek.

To her astonishment, the eyelid was intact. As if the sword had just skimmed it. There was nothing to warrant the patch he'd worn all these months. The linen had covered half his face.

She'd expected something deeper. Something dark. An emptiness where his eye should be. Instead the scar simply swiped across his eyelid like a strong wind. His eye was there, and with both eyes closed they...*matched*.

'How?' she whispered.

'I cannot open the lid. I cannot blink.'

'Can you see with it?'

'My sight is gone. Something else severed that I cannot get back.'

'Why cover it? It's—'

'Repulsive.'

The word was so far from the truth. 'Hardly even nicked.'

'Nicked?'

He gave a soft huff of breath, as if that simple word had hit him. And she knew it had, seeing the way hearing it had softened his gaze even more.

'I haven't worn a patch for years. Only when it was healing. In my line of business my injury is an asset.'

'Because you look fearsome?'

There was pleased curve to his lips. 'Because they underestimate me. They look at it as a weakness.'

She didn't understand. There was nothing weak about Nicholas.

Something flashed in his expression. 'And yet *you* don't see me that way.'

She shrugged. When she had first seen the scar, she'd only thought of his pain. What he'd endured without her. But to think of this man with any weakness was beyond her comprehension.

Another curve to his lips, a similar shrug to hers. 'So simple—but I don't understand. You have to know I don't.'

She'd have to explain. '*Look* at you.'

She gestured with her hands, indicating the breadth of his shoulders, his height like that of no man she'd ever known, those arms that could control a team of oxen through boulders. Arms that could hold a female close.

'What do you see?' he insisted.

There was no mischief or amusement on his part at seeing her vague hand gestures. He truly wanted to know what she saw in him.

She laid her palm against his cheek, traced her fingers along the thin, jagged seam of his scar. It was softer than it looked. Contrasting with the stubble of his jaw so roughly shaved.

'If I were a mercenary meeting you on a battlefield…' Sword arm raised, all his strength and training engaged, menace and lethality in his gaze. 'I'd think you were dangerous.'

He stilled her hand with his own. A tender touch that somehow made her heart beat faster.

'I can barely fathom that life you had, so...' She shrugged again. 'Since it's me, I just see *you*, Nicholas. All these months I've wanted to see more of you. I *hate* this scrap covering you.' She opened her hand and let the linen flutter to the ground. 'I don't want it back. Not here. Not... anywhere.'

There was a flare of light, of hope, before his expression darkened again. 'It's worse elsewhere. The scar...the injury...far worse. Because it was an upward stroke.'

She couldn't imagine it being worse, or what he must have suffered. She hurt simply thinking of his pain. What he continued to suffer because others treated him differently until they knew better.

Bracing herself, knowing how much she would hurt for him at what she might see, she nodded.

She wanted this moment with him because Nicholas was...just him. And if he could be brave enough to reveal whatever he seemed reluctant to show her, she could be brave enough to see it.

He looked to the right and the left, then huffed out a breath before he gripped the back of his tunic and tore it off.

A sound escaped her suddenly closed throat. There was no word to describe the scar cutting wide across his abdomen, becoming thinner as it arced up over his chest. Deep. Jagged. As if someone had carved him.

It didn't match the scar across his face. Not in depth, width, or even in direction. Not the clean sweep of an upward stroke, as he'd suggested. This was… This was as if the sword had pierced him and he'd turned his body to fling it out of the way.

But the blade had sunk deep. And when he'd turned… Her eyes followed the scar up. When he had turned it had gouged his body. A great uneven furrow, with the certainty of pain and agony.

There was a roar in her ears as she followed the scar's path up his body. Suddenly she was there with him. Right beside Nicholas as he slashed his enemies on the battlefield.

She almost felt a heavy cold mist that did nothing to cool the heat of fear and strength rushing through her limbs. She heard the clash of metal, horses screaming, men crying out in victory and loss.

This wasn't an injury. Something a man—a body—would recover from. This was permanent damage. Unending pain.

How could he have withstood it? How could any man, even one of his size? Any lesser and he'd be dead. He *should* be dead. There, where the scar went across his heart, it bisected his torso as thoroughly as a butcher.

He had been butchered on the battlefield. It was as if she had been there. Felt it. Heard it.

A large hand was encircling her arm. Shaking her until her eyes went to his. His gaze was fierce, his lips were moving, but she didn't hear his words—heard only the battle that raged on in her head until there were different cries of agony.

Trembling… Shaking… But nothing like that

moment when her horse had slipped and she had thought she would hurtle to the ground. That moment of realisation of fear of terror.

He pulled until she was held in his arms. Held securely, a heartbeat steady against her chest. *His* heartbeat. Then his voice. Scraps of words. Her name. Apologies. Soft murmurings. Comforting her until she rested against him.

She could hear his heart beat more strongly now. The sounds of the battle were fading. She rested her hand on his chest. Felt that he was alive under his healed wound. He was *alive*.

'There you are.' He curled his fingers under her chin and brought her gaze to his.

Tenderness. Concern.

'I'm so sorry,' she whispered.

She was aware that she was held against this man's naked chest. That they'd shared kisses. He pressed her close and she could feel the rigid length of him. The need of him. And how she wanted more. *Everything.*

That want was still there underneath, juddering under her too-tight skin with emotions she couldn't seem to contain. Touching him helped.

Touching him brought her back to this time, *now*, and to his kisses. The way his tongue delicately licked, his breath caressed her ear.

'That's twice now,' he murmured. 'Twice you've scared me. I'm a mercenary, Matilda. If this gets out you'll have no—'

Wanting to feel him again, she rubbed at his chest. He huffed out a breath. Tracked her hand on him with his gaze.

'What is it you need?' His voice was almost a growl.

She loved the smattering of hair beneath her palm, the unyielding body underneath. The warmth of him in the chill air. This calmed her. This was the truth of Nicholas alive.

'I'm so sorry. I don't know what happened. One moment I was here…' She shook her head. 'And then I was there with you. There in Spain. I was beside you and I saw this happen.'

His lips parted. There was a flash of pain and need, then he slowly nodded. 'You were there?'

Oh. No comfort now. None.

She had been there in his thoughts when his enemy had gouged his body. In his thoughts when he'd received that letter telling him she'd married another. He'd received this scar and she had hurt him again. How could he forgive her? How could he *want* her?

She removed her hand, tried to step back.

He grabbed her elbows, held her firmly. Ducked his head so she would see everything he felt. There was so much there…

'No. Don't,' he said.

She shook her head, her eyes darting.

'Don't think of that. Not now.' He gave a little shake to her elbows when she tried to pull free. 'Enough separates us. No more.'

'But—'

'Do you want me?' he said. 'Still? Like this? With this?'

Want him? Want his strength? His resolve and determination? The intoxicating heat and scent of his body?

She saw the way his gaze searched hers. The scar which furrowed into the very element of him. Nicholas was here. Alive and holding her. The scar was simply him.

Did she want him?

'Desperately.'

His calloused hands cradled her jaw, lifted her

chin. A brush of his lips. Dry. Firm. Another kiss. Deeper. Harder. More insistent as his arms went around her. He trailed his kisses along her jaw, down her neck, behind her ear, where he already knew she was sensitive.

She gasped. He gave a rough chuckle, but it was her turn next. His tunic was off and she could play and touch wherever she wanted. And she did want.

It was different this time. Not just the scar, but what was underneath. Despite his training, and earning his knighthood, he hadn't been honed like he was now. His body was different, its muscles and sinews distinguished; a topography of a warrior's form. His skin was burnished from many years in the sun. His years and experience had defined him until he was…*more* than he had been six years ago. So much more.

Her eyes couldn't take in enough, and she lifted her gaze to his. His expression was bemused, as if he couldn't believe his fortune.

'You're different,' she said.

'The longer you do that, the more I'll be changing.'

She was skimming her palm and fingers along

his chest, as if there were paths for her to follow. She could feel that in the beat of his heart, the raggedness of his breath.

The tension between them was tightening.

Heat rushed her skin—not out of embarrassment, but because she knew what he meant.

'Oh, you find that humorous?' he said, his voice deepening.

Was she smiling? Maybe a little. His body was rugged and yet honed like a sword. She didn't know what to expect under his other clothes. She'd watched him carry timber for houses, plough the fields, train with sword and shield, but nothing had ever been revealed to her.

'My lips curve not in humour,' she said, not surprised her voice sounded husky.

The weather was chilly, and cool air prickled along her neck and along his skin as well. But the weather didn't account for the increased sensitivity of her skin. It was seeing him.

Now she could see why his body moved so fluidly—why it seemed his weaponry was an extension of him. Because his body *was* a weapon.

'Why *do* your lips curve, then?' The tip of

his blunt finger brushed across her jawline to her lips.

Now she saw him with a woman's eye, how could she not smile in appreciation?

More touch. Along the dips of his shoulders, flattening her palms against his chest to feel more of him. Exploring. Noting the roughness of his hair, the sensitive skin underneath. The cords and ridges of his abdomen. Watching the muscles tense and flex under her light touch.

'I like this,' she said.

'So do I—too much. It's my turn.'

She was untying the ribbons at her sides before he had even gripped her gown. Her arms were in the air before he began to tug it over her head. He threw it over a fallen tree.

Now only in her loose chemise, she kept her arms up to help him with that garment as well. Instead, he gripped the fabric and pulled it up to her hips. Locking his hands, he shoved his thigh between her legs.

When he languidly pressed his thigh against her, her head fell forward and she gripped his shoulders while he supported her. She wanted more touch, wanted him to rip the chemise from her.

'I want to feel you,' she whispered.

'Me you, as well. Except we're out in the open and it's cold.'

'I don't feel the cold.'

He scowled at that. 'I don't want anyone seeing you. Us. I won't share.'

She gripped his face. Tried to make sense of it all. 'Is there someone near?'

'I can hear nothing, see nothing, but you.'

She had ridden hard and far, and he had followed her. This deep in the woods there shouldn't be anyone. No hunting this late in the day, no reason to be here during this part of the year.

Still, she tried to look.

He gently cupped her face with his big hand and pulled her lips to his. A brush against her lower lip. Then a firmer one, pulling in her upper lip before he licked along the seam.

'No thinking. No waiting. I'll have you like this. I need you like this. Out in the open. Not slow. I'm frantic for you, Matilda.'

He rubbed his hands along her sides. Skimmed

his knuckles over her breasts. Strummed his thumbs over her as he breathed across the tips.

'I ache...'

He rocked his hips forward against hers. 'Yes!'

She wanted. Needed. She pulled her chemise off.

Nicholas fell to his knees. Pulled her to him and rested his head against her stomach. His fingers splayed on her ribs. Grappling at his hips, he felt it, tried to hold it back. The taste of her on his lips was driving him forward as much as the feeling of her against him.

'Please...' she begged.

Her lips parted in invitation and he took them, dipped his tongue inside. There was a tangle of tongues as her hips moved, seeking and finding him. And then on a rough groan he sank deep into her.

Then there was nothing but this—her sounds, the clenching of her hands on his hips, her legs rubbing against his. Shuddering, he pulled out, held steady until her eyes opened. He never wanted this to end. Wanted to feel her clenching him again and again before this ended.

Matilda pinned him with the need and desire in her mesmerising eyes. Never wanting to close his own gaze, needing to capture everything she felt over and over, he drove into her again and again.

'Nicholas…'

Her body was arching under him. Taut like a bow. How many times had he envisaged this? The curls of her hair damp against the green grass. The flush of her skin. Her nipples puckered and red from his kisses. Peaking and asking for more.

But the way she felt against him… Her willowy figure lithe and strung tight. Never had he envisaged this. For she was so much more, and his body prepared, tightened for her.

Too soon.

It was her response. The vision of her beneath him. He drew his nails into his palms, bit the inside of his mouth. The sharp pain did nothing to stop what they'd started, what his body demanded he finish with his release.

Too soon.

'Don't move,' he said.

Her eyes flew open. Her gaze taking in his loss of control. The slick sweat sliding down his neck. His breath ragged. Past spent. His every sense centred to her. His hips aching for one strong thrust.

Her eyes darkened. Her glowing skin was burnished to gold. Her lips parted to hasten her increasingly shallow breaths. The restlessness of her legs scrabbled against his, against the grass they lay on. Trying to find purchase. To *move*.

When he gripped her hips to hold her still, her core fluttered, then grew stronger.

'Don't—' He groaned, his head bowing in defeat even as he struggled to last.

'Please...' Her hands were stroking against his shoulders, his arms, moving down to his hands then back up again. She was desperate to make him move.

'Matilda,' he rasped. 'I can't—'

His grip stilled her body, but he could do nothing about her limbs. Her stroking hands were now frantically slapping against his wet shoulder blades, his back. Her feet had found purchase, flat on the ground so she could draw up her knees sharply beside him. Sprung tight. Her core gaining purchase, her pulls growing stronger.

So long he had waited for her. He never wanted this to end.

'Wait…' he begged.

'Now!' she demanded.

She knew what she needed. What they both needed. Sinking her nails into his shoulders and ramming herself upward, she cried out her release as her core tugged him into her body, into the heat of her.

He was lost. Gripping her tight, thrusting deep, he bowed his body over hers and roared her name.

Moments later they were catching their breath. Completely bared to the elements. The cold breeze, the birds in the trees. The grass still wet from the morning, the sun not warm enough to heat the earth they lay on.

Chilled, despite Nicholas's arms around her, Matilda burrowed closer to him. Revelled in the exhalation of his breath, the sound he made that sounded close to one of contentment. Her body ached, but in a way it never had before. Replete. Relaxed. Whole. She was truly whole after so much emptiness.

Yet there was something just under her skin, thrumming under the even beat of her heart and her breath. Pricking between her languid thoughts of the way Nicholas had made love to her.

Words she had heard many years ago.

The feel of his body should have lent them truth. Yet somehow what they'd shared didn't feel like the truth. And it was that thought she followed more than those that made her feel rested. She followed the pricks and jabs to her conscience.

The reasons she hadn't told Nicholas that she loved him—she remembered them. Now that they had shared their kisses and caresses. She'd realised too late, because she had confessed too much in the way she'd held him, kissed him. Made love to him.

Because she knew that, as much as they had shared, there was one fact that remained. One fact they still didn't share. That had torn them apart all those years ago. He had left because he was restless. Because Mei Solis hadn't been enough for him.

That fact hadn't changed. Mei Solis was still a farm and a manor. Nicholas was still a knight. And no matter how many kisses, caresses and professed words of love, there was nothing here that would make him stay.

That thought jabbed at her soul, but she didn't want to think on it. Not now that Nicholas's exploring caresses were sending shivers along her thighs. Never as she bared her neck to welcome his kisses and tugged him to her.

Chapter Fourteen

Nicholas shifted in place to ease the familiar sting of training. Tomorrow his back would ache from the swinging of his sword, and fresh bruises would appear. Even so, it had been a successful day; his hands hadn't cracked and he had suffered no wounds.

A good day for his men as well, as they'd laughed and kept score. Slapping shoulders over the few victories, bonding in the many losses.

Mei Solis might be an agricultural manor, but over the years wealth had been built up here. So Nicholas had sent many men here to train and protect. Men who had carried his coin and his messages to Louve. Who'd stayed on for protection for the required period of time to pay a debt or earn coin of their own. Some had remained after their agreed time, and those Louve had ensured continued their training...or they had trained him.

Louve rolled his left shoulder over and over, and Nicholas smirked.

'He almost took my arm off,' Louve grumbled, though his expression was admiring. It was rare someone got one up on him.

'Your fault for turning when he had a hold of his sword like that.'

'Took my chance.'

'To dislocate your shoulder?'

'To make that Spanish bastard feel more pain than I will tomorrow.'

'Ah, Graviel never did fight fair.'

'Still doesn't.'

'If he lasted with you, you must have trained him well. He wanted to be a mercenary but had not enough experience.'

'So you sent him here to break my arm?'

'Someone needed to do it.'

Nicholas was pleased that Mei Solis had men who could provide protection. Not enough men—but then Mei Solis wasn't the grand castle of his grandfather's dream, it was a farm. With good, useful lands not only to make him wealthy, but to help the people who tilled it.

In that way it was better than his grandfather's ambitions for a grand castle. Mei Solis was more than a family's vanity.

Nicholas glanced to the sky. Soon he'd have to call a halt to the training and get on with his other duties at Mei Solis. What he *wanted* to do was return to Matilda's bed and stay there for days.

He couldn't help but wonder what she was doing and how Julianna fared. The days were still cold, despite the early spring. But most days now held warmer winds, and in a couple more weeks they'd see each other out in the fields.

Never before had he taken such care with the land. Now his days were inundated with tenants, wanting discussions over flagons of ale. He might have coin to pay for supplies, but the future of Mei Solis depended on the prosperity of its crops. The future for Matilda and Julianna depended on the manor.

Temporary? Nothing he'd done since that moment Matilda had ridden to the jumping field had been temporary.

A fortnight had passed since that time in the field. The days and nights since then had been full of stolen glances. Kisses in stairwells and against doors. Wanting more and taking it. Their private rooms were separate from the rest of the manor. Ideal for the nights.

But always, *always* she came to him in his room and then left. He had had two weeks of trying to capture her attention in the hall or in the village, only to have her turn away.

For the most part, he'd let her. But there had been moments when he had stopped her leaving, when he had grabbed her wrist or touched her arm. Asked her if she was well, if it was all too much, if she wanted to stop.

Though her eyes were always filled with unsaid conflicting emotions, her words and her actions were always the same. Words of acceptance and encouragement. A curve to her lips and a light to her eyes, indicating how much she still wanted this. Wanted *them*.

He wanted to believe her, but lingering was

the fact that although he had said he loved her, she'd never repeated those words to him.

He'd talk of future seasons together, and what he wanted to do for her, Julianna and Mei Solis, but she'd grow quiet.

He argued with himself that she needed time. Roger had died less than a year ago, and she was caring for Julianna, still lacking asleep. And she was now getting even less sleep, since he never denied her when she came to his bed.

He was greedy for her now that he could kiss her, talk to her in the quiet hours as she fed Julianna, feel her hair against his shoulder and the length of her legs against him, even if she never stayed the whole night. So, needing to be near her, he didn't want to know the truth.

He never pushed her. Let her set the pace. Let her keep the secret of them. That was what he was. He was her secret.

'And there you go again!' Louve laughed.

Nicholas pulled reluctantly from his thoughts. 'Where do I go?'

'You didn't hear any of my words, did you?' Louve shook his head. 'Men in love are useless.

Every one of you. No wonder you left yourself wide open and took that fist to your ribs.'

Men in love? Was he that obvious?

'You think I can't recognise the signs?' asked Louve. 'Your eyes search the grounds when you're not occupied at your tasks. You look for her every day, just like I look for Mary.'

Louve had confessed to loving Mary, but other than seeing Louve entering her home, Nicholas had seen no love there. Only something that occurred behind closed doors. Like a secret.

Except everyone in Mei Solis knew that Louve visited Mary, and that there was nothing more. No betrothal or promises, nor even loving smiles.

'She's not good enough for you.'

Louve's eyebrows shot up. 'Shouldn't *I* know the truth of that?'

'Not in this.'

At Louve's questioning gaze, Nicholas went on.

'I've earned the truth of it.' He had—with his and Matilda's trials. They'd loved in the past, and they loved now. He knew all the sides of that emotion, and no doubt he'd learn some more.

'Perhaps you're right,' Louve said. 'But—'

'And you're my friend.'

'Always—even though you've known of this for months and haven't said anything before.'

Because he was here only temporarily. He was supposed to leave. It was spring. After the winter he had meant to leave.

He'd told Matilda he loved her, but Matilda hadn't said it back. Was he no better than Louve?

'You can do better,' he insisted.

Louve's eyes were careful, assessing. 'You really *do* love her. What would you have done if Roger hadn't died?'

'Continued to love her and found joy in the fact that she chose the better man.'

'Does she know everything?'

'Too soon,' he said.

He might not be able to keep from touching her, and he knew she cared for him, but love? She was only now grieving Roger's death; had only just given birth to their daughter.

Asking anything more from her would be greedy, even for him. Which meant he would respect Matilda and give her whatever she needed.

If she needed time, or to keep their relationship secret, he'd give that to her.

Mary's situation was different, since her husband had been gone for years. 'It's not too late for you,' he said.

Louve's expression eased. 'It never has been.'

'If so, then—'

There came a pounding of hooves and the distinct clatter of metal. Shouts and the low reverberations of voices. Many voices.

Nicholas and Louve turned to the gates.

'Who could—?' Louve said, his strides matching Nicholas's.

Both hastened their steps as the sounds grew more chaotic. The voices were loud, with the unmistakable sound of horses and the creak of leather.

Closer Nicholas's footsteps took him to the gates. But he didn't need to see the man who was surrounded by ten others. He needed to see the banner that was raised.

Reynold of the Warstone family was here.

Chapter Fifteen

'Here, Father. Sit here.' Matilda bore her father's weight across the small room and gently eased him into the chair.

'Why is there fire?'

'It's not yet spring. Not so many fires outside, only inside, and we need this one for food. Can you leave it alone? Aren't you hungry?'

'She's a good baby,' Holgar said.

Julianna was wide awake, her sweet gaze taking everything in. Her hair and eyes were so much like Roger's it made her heart ache, but there was also joy in seeing them. Acceptance as well.

Matilda looked at her father, who was no longer looking at her or the baby but at the fire again. Always the fire. She might not understand where her father went in his thoughts, but there were times when she almost understood him. When she looked at the fire she thought of her mother as well. Of her small frame, her hands perpetually cold, perpetually reaching towards the flames to warm them. Those were happy thoughts, even though she missed her mother.

'You were a good baby,' he said.

Matilda's eyes pricked. 'I was?'

His eyes glanced at her and her heart stopped. Then he swung his gaze away. 'Not enough fires outside.'

'It's nearly spring,' she whispered.

'That's good,' he said, nodding.

Matilda couldn't get her heart to work normally. A tight fist had squeezed around it in that moment when he'd seen her and she him. It was gone now, but the feeling of warmth and joy was still there. His love for her was there underneath.

'It *is* good,' she told him.

A quick knock at the door made her jump.

'It's me!' Bess said striding in. 'I thought you'd be here if you weren't at the manor.'

She tilted her head. 'Father keeps returning here.'

Bess glanced around and looked at the low fire. 'That'll be difficult until spring.'

Their house was separated from the rest of the huts. Roger had always been out in the fields with everyone, glad of his privacy in the evenings. Except a house too private with fire to keep it warm would mean her father might not be safe.

'I like to think of him here.'

There were happy memories here—fresh and new joy surrounding them like the warmer winds and the longer hours of sunshine. Like a father and a daughter's love.

Bess gave her usual efficient nod. 'We'll make certain someone is here with him, then.'

Her father was alive, in her home, and would have care; she couldn't ask for anything more. However, *her* worries weren't what had caused her friend's hands to be clasped so tightly.

'What has brought you here?'

'There's trouble.'

Matilda glanced at her father, who still gazed at the fire and didn't move. 'What is the matter?'

'There are a lot of men at the gates.'

Matilda stood and bounced Julianna. 'From what manor?'

'No manor. I've never seen them before, but Nicholas has. He's greeted them, and is now walking with their leader to the Great Hall.'

'We have visitors and they'll need food.'

Those were her duties—ones she enjoyed. Already her thoughts were moving to how best to provide. Wondering, too, what manner of men these friends of Nicholas's were.

'I don't know how much hospitality they'll want. They look like trouble,' Bess said, reaching out to take Julianna.

'She's fed.' Matilda handed her over. 'If they're men who are Nicholas's acquaintances and have come to visit, what could possibly be the trouble?'

'When you see Nicholas's expression you'll understand.'

All was clear the moment she strode into the hushed hall.

She'd changed her dress, plaited her hair. Any signs of taking care of her father and Julianna all morning were gone. Not that she cared for her appearance in a vain sense. She knew only that Bess's description meant she needed to present a solid persona with no weakness.

It had taken her some time to get ready, so she'd expected the ale to be flowing and the conversation to be lively. But as the hall's door closed behind her she was sorry she'd spared those few moments, for though Nicholas clearly knew them, these men weren't friends.

Around a dozen men stood, while one other sat with Nicholas near the fire at the end of the hall. The men were clean, with clothes made of fabrics much finer than hers. They looked like men who had been the victors in every battle they'd ever fought. Except for the man with Nicholas they were all standing ominously silent and eerily still even as their eyes roved the hall, all its contents and its persons.

Yet even those seemingly innocent looks seethed with an undercurrent. As if each man was analysing exactly how to kill everyone in the room and what goods would be best to steal.

These men reminded her of how Nicholas had been when he'd first strode back into to Mei Solis. Mercenaries. Lethal. Over six months Nicholas had been here now, and she'd almost forgotten the dark edge that he had worn. He had softened since then, as if something had eased within him.

Not so this leader, the man talking quietly with Nicholas now. He was something else altogether.

His body was at ease, his mannerisms refined and civilised as he gestured over some story he told. Whatever it was amused him, and also Nicholas, for he returned the man's laughter with a tight smile.

The man wore all black. His hair was dark, his skin well bronzed. He had no false air of confidence, but the bored demeanour of someone who had seen it all before and was weary.

Because of that he seemed the deadliest of all. A bored man surrounded by trained warriors was a man capable of massacring the inhabitants of Mei Solis and then slicing the necks of his own men.

Slowly, steadily, she approached Nicholas, who turned to acknowledge her even while his expression was almost flat, his eye giving no indication of his thoughts.

The man turned as well, still laughing, and looked expectant. 'And who is this?'

'This is Matilda, who has been caring for the manor and the contents of its larder in my absence.'

The man gestured with his cup. 'Then I have her to thank for this fine ale.'

'Indeed.' Nicholas indicated the man at his side. 'Reynold from the Warstone family and his men have paid me a visit.'

No introductions, but names exchanged. Which meant Nicholas wanted her to know who this man was. His name wasn't familiar, and she had never seen him before. However, there were some clues in the quietness of the hall, in the men who exchanged glances with each other as this brief conversation drew on.

Nicholas avoided looking at her. Taking her

cue from him, she gave a formal nod of greeting. 'Will you need a repast?'

'Yes.'

The coldness in Nicholas's tone sent fear down her spine. These men weren't friends at all. Keeping her hands steady and her expression neutral, she asked, 'And accommodations?'

Nicholas turned his head to Reynold, lifting a brow.

Reynold's lips curved. A fox who already had the hen in its mouth. 'Most definitely.'

The only indication that Nicholas didn't like that news was a shift in his body and the relaxing of his hand at his side. The movement was slight, but enough that it freed the sword pinned at his side—as if he might need it at any moment, or was envisaging using it.

Matilda kept her eyes evenly on Reynold of Warstone and nodded her head. 'That is very good. Then if you'll permit me to see to your food and lodgings…?'

Nicholas, still not glancing her way, waved his hand.

Nicholas didn't even exhale. He would do

nothing to indicate weakness, and Matilda was his absolute weakest point.

The room was now empty of servants, or anyone who mattered to him. Louve would be preparing the men, if it came to that.

Louve hadn't been pleased to be dismissed. However, there had been no time for any other preventative measures. He had to face Reynold alone.

If Reynold wanted him dead, there were easier ways of doing it than meeting him on his home turf. Reynold was here for other reasons. He simply needed to know what they were.

'I didn't expect to see you so soon.'

Reynold grabbed the flagon to refill his goblet. 'Yet you expected me.'

'You let Rhain go with an open invitation.'

'Doesn't that mean *Rhain* expected me?'

Nicholas twirled the cup in his hand when he truly wanted to pace. However, his movements would be tracked by Reynold's guardsmen. At least in this part of the hall their conversation wouldn't be overheard.

'Rhain argued such—but then he always had an inflated sense of his own worth.'

Nicholas was glad that he was right and his friend was wrong. Reynold had sought him first for revenge. Nicholas would finally face the man who'd threatened his friends. Rhain had always wanted to be the protector, when in fact it was Nicholas's duty. Rhain outranked him as a man and as nobility.

'And what did you argue to him?'

'That he had Helissent and you wouldn't harm her.'

'That I would stop my threats to the mercenary who killed my brother? That scarred maiden has no worth to the Warstone family. No wealth, no connections.'

'You forget I travelled with her. Her worth is more than the Warstone family…and you know it.'

'It's true her cakes are sublime.' Reynold took a sip of his ale.

'So, no visits to Rhain since we…parted?'

'I have been too busy. Dead brother and all.'

Reynold could play with Nicholas all he

wanted—as long as he played only with him. Never with Matilda. How much time did he have while she prepared the repast and ensured accommodations? Not long enough. She would return. Reynold had seen her and would expect it.

'She was attractive,' Reynold said abruptly.

Nicholas faced his enemy. 'Helissent married Rhain.'

Reynold lifted his index finger from his cup. An indication of wanting to make his point. 'I meant your…server. Matilda.'

Nicholas forced a bored mien, though his insides roiled. He knew he had given no outward indication of his concern for her, but he *had* been thinking of her. Had a straying glance betrayed him?

'She's recently widowed with a babe.'

'How old is the babe?'

He didn't like the path of that question. There was no reason for Reynold to care how old Julianna was unless she was newly born and the mother was useless to a man. If Reynold stayed the night he'd know the truth.

'I believe four months.'

'Ah.'

That sounded too self-satisfied. He couldn't let it go—a warning must be laid out. 'Her late husband was one of my closest friends.'

'That must be awkward for you.'

'He would expect me to warn you.'

'And so I am well warned. Did you warn *yourself* before you lay with her?'

Spies. That wasn't possible—not here. Reynold couldn't have reached Mei Solis before he had arrived, but how else would he know of his relationship with Matilda?

Except for the messengers who had brought his coin and his instructions to Louve, Nicholas had grown up with every tenant here. Who could possibly be sending messages to Reynold? And why?

He had to stop his spinning thoughts. The Warstone family couldn't have any interest in him or his family. An impoverished knight with a wreck of a manor was of no use to Reynold.

Reynold laughed. 'One eye, and a scar that hides most of your features, and still you can't keep your thoughts to yourself. There are no spies here—it was simply your own actions. You were too careful with her. Your friend Rhain was the same with Helissent. Honestly, I can find *no one* to match me in immorality. Where is a decent liar these days?'

'Maybe you should look to your own family.'

'Guy was a blundering, spoiled fool.'

'You have more brothers.'

'Two—who have the subtlety of a battering ram.'

'A very powerful ram.'

Reynold stood and pointed his finger again. 'Maybe it is you who spy on me?'

Anyone who had trained at Edward's court knew of the Warstone family. Only a handful of families had the ear, wealth and power of a kingdom without owning a country. Even more, the Warstone family had an edge over all those truths. They had the loyalty of the King, and never, ever could be crossed.

Reynold didn't have an inflated sense of his worth. He knew *exactly* what he was worth. The man was clever, wealthy by his own hand and, if rumour be believed, as lethal as the legend of

Black Roger—King Edward's right-hand knight for many years.

In other words, he was not a man to cross. Not even a man to know.

Nicholas had a dagger in his belt and he knew the reach of his arm. His height was to his advantage. He could strike Reynold long before he tried something.

'What are you doing here, Reynold?'

The man looked out at the clouds in the sky and then off across the fields to the horizon. 'I haven't been to this part of the country in a long time and I thought I'd visit.'

'You've *never* been to this part of the country.'

'True, but I am long overdue. It seems beautiful—and very empty.'

How much time did he have before Reynold made his move? Whatever it was, it needed to be done soon. Servants would soon bring food. Even now he could smell it and hear the clattering of dishes.

'Take your revenge—or whatever it is you need to do.'

'Can't we dine first?'

'Is that why you're here? Because you're hungry? Then I will feed you, and you can be on your way.'

'I've travelled far.'

Nicholas just held back a retort. Reynold was playing a game. 'Then you'll stay for the night. But know that this is the only moment you have to tell me what you must.'

Reynold lifted a sardonic brow. 'Because of the woman?'

'Because I am busy.'

'You expect me to leave on the morrow? When I'm expecting to stay for a week?'

Nicholas had no time for games. Mei Solis was as all-encompassing as he remembered, and he still hadn't discovered the reason for Matilda's troubled gaze.

If Reynold stayed he would discover how tenuous a hold he had on his property, and on the woman he loved. Reynold and his games could shove a wedge between him and all his intentions for the future here.

Reynold could try, but Nicholas would see

him dead before he caused any malcontent in his own home.

'You intend to stay a week?' Nicholas said. 'What a welcome surprise.'

It was far into the night when she heard Nicholas's heavy steps up the staircase and down the corridor. The tell-tale creak of his door and its closing. It was the sound Matilda always listened for. The time of night she'd meet him in his room.

Not knowing what to expect tonight, she didn't immediately walk to his room, even though Julianna slept peacefully in her cradle. She stood in indecision and hated it. Years of being her own mistress and this was what she was reduced to—mincing around as if she didn't know her own mind. She *did* know. She wanted Nicholas.

Quietly, though no one should hear anything from this private corridor, she sneaked into Nicholas's room. Instead of undressing for the night, he was sitting on his bed, his head in his hands.

'You shouldn't be here tonight,' he said, though he didn't raise his head.

She didn't have to listen to his cutting words—especially when they didn't matter. 'I want to be here.'

'Reynold will know you're here.'

'He most likely already knows my room is next to yours and has assumed.'

Nicholas dropped his hands and rested his elbows on his knees. His hair was loose and tangled about his face. Even after a hard day's labour, she'd never seen Nicholas look so exhausted.

'Reynold hasn't assumed. He knows because I accidentally told him.' Standing impatiently, he looked about the room as if for something to do. 'He knows everything. Always. It isn't just his wealth that makes him dangerous.'

She'd never seen Nicholas unsure before. Even when he was restless, he was indomitable. Assured. 'You told me that you and Rhain barely escaped with your lives. I assumed it was because of clashing swords.'

He shook his head slowly. 'You're dead before Reynold ever draws his sword.'

The full truth of the matter hit her. Nicholas

had had some play in the cause of Reynold's brother's death. Reynold hadn't exacted his revenge, and now he was here. He was here and he knew of her relationship with Nicholas.

'He'll harm Julianna?'

Nicholas's restlessness stopped, and he turned to her almost violently. 'He won't. And he won't touch you either.'

'Yet you said he kills before he draws his sword. You won't see him make his decision or hear him give the order. In the middle of night he could—'

Nicholas grabbed her arms and pulled her closer. Power, strength, comfort reverberated from every ounce of him, and she took it.

'A man like Reynold likes games more than executions or killing children,' he said.

'What if he is finished playing his games?'

'Nothing and no one will harm you or Julianna.' He tilted his head, caught her eyes. 'I swear it,' he said, more powerfully than a vow.

Chapter Sixteen

Too polite. That was what Nicholas thought as he showed Reynold his estate the next day. They rode together as if they were amiable neighbours. The only thing that disputed this idyllic scene was the movement of Reynold's men, who had dispersed themselves farther afield. They were no longer guarding Reynold but roaming the entirety of Mei Solis—from the outer fields to the tenants' homes.

If they damaged crops or dirtied a kitchen floor with their boots he'd hear about it later.

If he was alive.

'The air is better here than in London.'

A remark about the weather—but Nicholas knew it for the threat it truly was.

'Did you come here from London?' he asked, as evenly as he could.

'Of course. I was following you and Rhain.'

'You should have ridden with us and kept us company.'

Reynold chuckled. 'That would have been entertaining.'

Knowing that Reynold would keep tabs on them had meant they'd trained hard along their way. The bastard probably knew that as well.

'I could have entertained you with my sword practice.'

'I haven't had training in so long...'

'I could accidentally skewer you.'

'Or I you.'

Not with Matilda and Julianna in danger. He was their shield now. If Reynold stepped out of place he'd be their sword as well.

'So what do you think of my humble home?'

'You want my opinion?'

'We could talk of the weather instead, or a training session between you and I that will never take place.'

'You like your home?' Reynold said.

'And the people in it.'

'I could tell you I will prove no threat, but I'd be lying.'

'At least you're trying to be honest.'

'I lied about following you from London.'

Nicholas shook his head and pulled his horse in front. Reynold caught up.

'I'm simply visiting…for now,' Reynold said.

'And when you're not visiting? What do you do here?'

'Not visiting? What else could I possibly do here out in the middle of nowhere?'

Another non-answer with one glaring fact: Reynold was staying and he had some agenda.

But, if so, Nicholas might as well get some use out of the extra man-power.

'Will you and your men help in the fields?'

'And let you near me with a plough?'

'You'd have one, too.'

'But *you* know how to use one.' Reynold gestured outwards. 'In all my imaginings, this isn't what I thought your home would be.'

Home. Mei Solis. Nicholas was beginning

to feel it just might be. 'What did you think it would be?'

'With you so scarred and tortured, I thought it would be dark. Grim. Instead it's comfortable and friendly.'

If he hadn't heard the hint of wistfulness behind Reynold's words he might have thought him to be dismissing his home.

The rest of the day was almost congenial. Reynold insisted on seeing every bit of the land and the manor, and Nicholas saw the benefit in not hiding anything. If Reynold wanted to see how he lived and where, he'd let him.

Nothing went unnoticed or untouched—from the gates and the ploughs, to the bars in the rooms below the Manor. Reynold seemed fascinated by each revealed facet.

For once Nicholas almost understood his interest. Now that Mei Solis wasn't falling apart, he, too, was appreciating the winding staircases, the odd additions, the uneven corridors and crooked cubbies.

When they returned to the manor's courtyard they were greeted with the domestic scene of

Bess jostling Julianna on her hip and Agnes skipping circles around them.

Matilda had some sort of stick in her hand and was drawing something in the air. Horses, no doubt.

The beauty of their happiness halted him, and he felt something somewhere in his chest before he could hide his reaction.

When he risked a glance to Reynold he knew it was too late to hide his joy. Reynold had seen everything.

Instead of commenting on it, he said, 'I think I'll rest before we dine tonight. If I may?'

Asking permission? Reynold had been giving orders since he'd arrived. Never anything overt enough to demand a challenge, but orders nevertheless. Nicholas had allowed it because there was too much at stake. One on one he knew he could take Reynold. The man wasn't soft, but he hadn't trained like Nicholas had…and nor did he have people to protect.

However, Reynold asking permission was something else. His expression gave nothing away. Respect? A trick? Something else to entertain himself with?

Whatever it was, Reynold had never done it before, and for that moment Nicholas almost admired him.

At his nod of agreement, Reynold guided his horse to the stables.

Feeding Julianna in the wee hours, in her bedroom, Matilda heard horses and tackle and the low murmurs of men. Holding her child, she glanced out of the window. Reynold and his men were fully dressed, fully packed, and looked ready to leave.

There were a few tenants milling about, and one of Nicholas's men at the gates, but the sun's light hadn't crested the horizon, which was still black. She heard nothing next door, and knew Nicholas slept.

Unlatching her baby, she adjusted her gown and rushed to his room. 'Wake up!'

Leaping from the bed completely naked, except for the sword at his side, Nicholas swept the room and then shoved her aside to scan the corridor.

'Well done for protecting me from *me*. I'm the one who woke you!'

With a question in his eyes, he turned to her. 'What is it?'

She didn't know whether to be amused or alarmed. Amusement won.

'What's funny?' he growled, as he set his sword on the bed and pulled on his tunic.

'Nothing, but you—' She pointed at him, then reined in her laughter. 'Reynold's leaving.

Nicholas grabbed his braies. 'It's only been four days.'

'What does that mean?'

'I'll find out.' He shoved on his breeches and boots and strode out to the hall.

Matilda clutched Julianna. She knew Reynold was leaving—what she didn't know was why he would leave without Nicholas. Nicholas had looked just as surprised as she. But that meant nothing.

Matilda returned to her room to stare out of the window. Bouncing Julianna on her hip, she watched the men in the courtyard below. The dim light and the distance prevented her from knowing what was being said or understanding anything of what was happening.

She knew nothing except that Nicholas was now fully dressed and talking with Reynold. From around the corner she could see Louve pulling two horses towards them. One was saddled, the other burdened with satchels.

'So this is it,' she said to Julianna. 'This is how he leaves. In the early morning, without saying goodbye. At least that is consistent. He didn't say goodbye last time either.'

Tears pricked her eyes and she dipped her head into Julianna's warm neck and inhaled her daughter's sweet scent. It didn't calm her heart.

His leaving was different this time. It hurt more and he hadn't yet walked out through the gates. Maybe it was worse because now she knew what it meant to miss Nicholas. Or maybe it was because she knew the cruelty of time and what it could take away.

Nicholas's eye. Roger's life.

Maybe it was because she loved him. Not with

the carelessness of a girl who didn't know the cost of a broken heart and betrayed trust. She loved him as a woman who knew what it meant to love through birth and death, through storms and warm rains.

When he walked through those gates again, to continue his mercenary life, she knew she wouldn't be able to weather it this time around. There would be no coming back.

All her fault. None of this would be unfolding before her if not for her misunderstanding. Her lack of trust in him.

Tucking Julianna under her neck, to feel her baby's soft breath and tender fingers against her skin, Matilda pulled in a ragged breath. She tried to remember that they had resolved their mistrust. It was true. Their trust was tentative, but it was there.

However, trust, unfortunately, didn't solve Nicholas's innate restlessness. Didn't change the fact that he didn't belong at Mei Solis and she did. The fact that she hadn't been enough to hold him here before, and she knew there was no guarantee now.

Pivoting away from the window, she marched to the bed. She was no girl, but a woman who knew what she wanted. This time she wouldn't let him leave without saying goodbye.

Gently prying Julianna's fingers from her gown, she stopped. What would happen if she flew down the stairs and out through the door with Julianna in her arms? There would be no one to take her. She'd have her precious baby with her as she faced a man whom she knew was dangerous and Nicholas, who might reject her.

Fighting with herself, she hesitated. The old Matilda would have flown down the steps and disregarded the danger. However, her years apart from Nicholas, the confidence she'd gained with settling disputes and her marriage to Roger had taught her other ways of confrontation.

There would be consequences to rushing into that courtyard. If Nicholas left now, because of threat or because of restlessness, she couldn't risk Julianna. She must stay here. And when Nicholas walked out through that gate she'd stand here while her heart broke, knowing she hadn't told him she loved him.

* * *

Four days. That was the thought that pounded through him as Nicholas took the stairs two at a time. Four days and Reynold had given no clue as to why he'd come or why he'd stayed. Why he and his men had walked the land as if they surveyed it.

There had been no threats. All had been cordial—almost friendly. Reynold's entire demeanour had been that of a visiting relative. Which went against him now slinking off in the early hours.

Murmurs, the creak of leather and the sound of horses pawing the ground reached him as he rushed through the Great Hall. There was no commotion nor swords being drawn. His own men hadn't raised the alarm. Which meant Reynold's leaving was as cordial as his arrival.

So why this early departure in the middle of the night? Three days short of his intended stay?

He turned the corner and there they were. Reynold already mounted, pointing his horse's hooves as he pulled his horse in circles.

Reynold really was leaving. He'd almost missed him—and if not for Matilda he would have.

Reynold turned fully then. For a moment he looked weary, and then his face assumed the genial mask it had worn for days.

'How polite that you are here to see us off.'

Reynold's men were all mounted, and they circled their leader. Their eyes were still scanning their surroundings, as they had been for days now. This time, however, most of them had had their hands on their sword pommels.

All was quiet. Not even Louve was up and about. This departure was early even by farming standards.

Something was wrong.

When he was almost beside Reynold, he stopped. He was definitely within striking distance. A swift kick from Reynold would hurt him. He didn't expect one. Physical retribution wasn't Reynold's style.

To prove that point Reynold kept his eerie calm. It infuriated Nicholas, especially since it appeared as if he was skulking off in the middle of the night like a man who had committed a crime.

'Has harm come to my manor?' he demanded.

'Not now that—' Reynold stopped. 'It's far too early for attacks—as you know. I wouldn't wish this hour on my enemy.'

Nicholas kept his gaze steady and Reynold matched him. He'd expected to see the usual amused light in Reynold's eyes, but there was none.

Nicholas believed him. Reynold's departure and his men's alertness meant something—and he intended to find out what. This was *his* land, and these were *his* people. This was the life he had chosen for himself. He didn't care how dangerous Reynold was or how powerful his family. If there was a threat here, he must know about it and eliminate it.

'Has harm come to *you*?' he asked.

Surprise flashed, then was quickly gone. 'No. I've simply been informed that my visit must be cut short.'

If harm was to come to Reynold it would be coming to Matilda and Julianna as well. And yet

Nicholas knew he asked not only wanting the safety of his family, but for Reynold as well. If it was true, he wasn't going to let Reynold evade his questioning.

'Who informed you?'

'You are one of the most intelligent men I've ever known—and yet you ask this question?'

Reynold had other men. Spies scouring the country and coming and going to his manor. It was a suspicion now confirmed, but he needed more answers without the games. Because more spies exchanging information meant more threat.

He grabbed Reynold's bridle and lethal eyes met his. He knew his gaze matched them. 'What do I have to prepare for, Reynold. What are you to drop on my lands and people?'

Reynold sighed. 'Whatever you need to know has been left in my comfortable rooms.'

Nicholas tossed the reins back. 'What have you left me? What trouble is coming here?'

Reynold looked at his men, heard the stirrings at the gate. 'Have you no sense of circumspection?'

'I blocked a sword with my face and body—

and yet you ask that question?' He mocked Reynold's own words. His scar was blatant evidence of his lack of caution. His words were blunt, his actions sharper yet. 'This is my home,' he said. 'I will not allow secrets here.'

Reynold's mask slipped. 'I envy you your home and your honesty—but, alas, I must take advantage of it.'

Nicholas heard familiar footsteps and Louve stepped into his peripheral vision. He led two horses: his own, fully saddled, and another that carried satchels.

He eyed Louve, but then returned his attention to Reynold. 'It looks like you're taking advantage of my friends as well.'

Reynold leaned over his horse. It was a casual movement, but one that afforded them more privacy from over-eager ears. Nicholas didn't wonder why Reynold hadn't simply dismounted to talk to him. Reynold was a tactician, and on his horse he had the upper hand.

'I take advantage of no man—only of circumstances. You and Louve will have a chat before I go. I left a letter along with some satchels of coin in my rooms. *My* coin. More than King Edward knows I have, but not as much as I've left in other locations.'

Of all threats, this wasn't one he'd ever guessed at. 'You left your silver here?'

'And gold…gems. There might be a crown or two as well.'

'Why?'

Reynold's expression grew hard. 'You owe me a debt.'

Nicholas wasn't a man to be intimidated by a mere gaze. 'I didn't kill your brother.'

'You aided it.'

True.

'Rhain owes me much more. I only ask you to keep my coins safe, well hidden and secret.'

Nicholas had believed Reynold when he'd said he'd left a king's ransom in his home. The man didn't say much, and his words could often be construed in unusual ways, yet when he did say something directly it was the truth. For example when he said he'd kill you…or you owed him a debt.

Reynold wanted Nicholas to protect some of

his wealth, which meant he had to hide it from someone. But Mei Solis had no advantage in hiding such wealth.

'My home isn't a fortress. There are no trained men here to protect such an amount. And you and I are enemies.'

Reynold smiled. 'Exactly.'

It was a simple request, and too easy in payment for the death of a brother. Reynold truly hadn't loved his brother. So he demanded this for a tactical reason. If examined from that angle, the request was brilliant and risky. No one would suspect such an amount here.

An easy request, a brilliant idea…but still a threat. 'Who will be looking for it?'

'No one *now*—but that is why I leave earlier than I wanted.'

Nicholas looked pointedly to Louve, who kept his gaze steady. His friend was leaving with Reynold. He pulled his thoughts back to the man staring down at him. His mask had returned.

'I can't guarantee there won't be trouble in the future, though,' Reynold continued.

'Is it the King?'

No amount of cunning or begging would be enough if King Edward stormed his land.

Reynold's eyes turned distant. 'It could be anyone.'

'Anyone' was a dangerous word and held too much trouble. Nicholas's only sane option would be to decline—but what would happen then? He still owed this dangerous man a debt—not to mention whoever backed the Warstone family. And that included the King.

He didn't know what the punishment would be. Reynold wasn't the type simply to kill him. Rumours abounded concerning Reynold's calculating cruelty. And now that he'd spent time with him, Nicholas believed the rumours. But if he had to accept, he'd have one caveat.

'Whatever this is, I won't risk Matilda.'

Reynold's brows rose. 'I wouldn't either.'

Nicholas paused. Did Reynold mean literally that he wouldn't risk Matilda, or only if he was in Nicholas's place? It didn't matter. The outcome was the same. But Nicholas believed the bastard that Matilda wouldn't be at risk. Still...

'I won't leave the treasures where they are. I

don't have funds to build a fortress, but I have an idea to hide it that may suffice.'

'Don't tell me.'

'I wasn't intending to.'

'You're not keeping it either.'

Nicholas almost laughed. 'I intend to live like the next man—and I also pay my debts. Will this be enough to release me from mine to you?'

It would be a relief not to look over his shoulder any more.

Reynold's brows drew in. 'I can't guarantee that either. I do take advantage of circumstances. And if not me, others might.'

There might still be danger at Mei Solis that threatened Matilda and Julianna. Reynold offered him no guarantees at all. Yet Nicholas's options were limited. He'd simply have to do everything in his power to protect them. Changes would have to be made—subtle ones, so no one was any the wiser.

Reynold canted his head. 'You'll do it?'

'Yes.'

'For me?'

'For Rhain.'

'Ah, loyalty and friendship. I envy you that as well.' Then Reynold chuckled. 'Your home now has secrets.'

It did. 'When will you return?' he bit out.

He didn't like secrets, and he didn't like this payment of his debt. No guarantees…the debt not truly paid off. Nothing but obligations and too much risk. No other options but to accept it.

Reynold's brother Guy had deserved to die. Matilda and Julianna didn't.

No one at Mei Solis did.

'I may never return,' Reynold said.

Nicholas didn't hide his surprise. Reynold *never* admitted to weakness, but he just had.

He was dividing his wealth and distributing it without the King's knowledge. He was doing it to protect it, so that he could keep it. If he didn't return for it, it meant he was incapable of doing so. Because he'd be dead.

Whatever he was doing was dangerous, and he was depending on the men around him… and now on *him*. The man who'd helped kill his brother. Was Reynold desperate? Or truly clever? It didn't matter. At the heart of the action was the truth.

'You're trusting me with this?'

'Of course. I know where you live, and...'

Reynold glanced up, and Nicholas followed his gaze. Matilda, holding Julianna, was standing at the window, watching them. At that distance she wouldn't hear them, and she had to be weary. He should have told her to sleep, that he'd tell her about this exchange in the morning.

Reynold returned his gaze. 'And because of her I know you intend to stay here.'

It was a threat, but Nicholas felt that wasn't the reason why Reynold was doing this. After four days, was he now this enigmatic man's *friend*? If so, he couldn't have very many. And a friendship with Reynold was something he'd never confess to.

More secrets.

Louve appeared to have some as well.

Nicholas glanced at his oldest friend. There was no smirk nor any concern in his expression. Nothing to indicate why he stood there, intending to leave. Had he been threatened?

Reynold straightened and shook his head. 'I can see you worry for him. Rest assured, he leaves a free man. His coming with me has nothing to do with my full coffers.'

Somehow Nicholas believed that, too. 'Are we finished?'

'As you wish.'

Reynold pulled his horse closer to the gates and his guardsmen followed. Louve slowly walked up and took his place, in front of Nicholas.

'You told me I should leave here,' Louve said, his voice low.

Reckless words. 'Tell me why now.'

Louve shrugged. 'It's time. You and I both know that.

'If that is true, why have you always argued with me and told me to stay?'

'That's just in my nature.' Louve smirked. 'Otherwise it is too boring around here.'

Nicholas's hand curled into a fist. He was certain he'd strike him for answers.

Louve took in that fist as he raised a brow. 'Again?'

'If I have to.'

Louve gave a curt nod. 'I have no desire to

leave my home for ever with a bruise marring my beauty.'

'So...?'

'I didn't leave before. I couldn't leave because you, Nicholas, Lord of Mei Solis, were intending to go. Despite your recent return. Despite your saying it was your home, I knew you never intended to stay here. Until I was certain you'd stay I couldn't go.'

'I never said I wanted to leave.'

Louve grunted. 'In your every action and every carefully spoken word, you did.'

Was he so transparent? After all this time? That didn't bode well if he was to hide a fortune's worth of coin against Reynold's unknown enemy. He hoped it wasn't the King.

'You know me too well,' he said.

'I also knew when you'd decided to stay before you did. I am glad you discovered that.'

'I haven't told her.'

'You'd better hurry. She's no longer at the window, and who knows what conclusions she's drawn?'

'You could have left alone.'

'But where would be the fun in that?'

'Reynold isn't entertaining.'

'You laughed at his tales as much as the rest of us.'

He'd choked on his laughter, surprised that Reynold could be droll like Louve.

'He's not your friend.'

'Nor is he my enemy.'

'He is manipulative, corrupt, and he'll kill you without a thought.'

'Then I won't be bored—and I'll have loads of other distractions.'

Nicholas knew Louve spoke of replacing Mary, who refused to give him her heart.

'There are other women.'

'There's no one here but her.'

'So you leave to find another?'

'I leave because it's time, and because Reynold will pay well. You've trained me, but he can train me in a different way. He's complicated, and I know my throat could be slit at any moment. That understanding will only hone my skills.'

'You wish to be a mercenary? Go to Rhain, then.'

'He trades only information. It's not enough.'

Louve was restless, and what he needed wasn't here, but that didn't mean his leaving was welcome.

'You'll be missed.'

'With certainty.'

Nicholas laughed. No need to exchange any words on whether there would be correspondence, or where Louve would be living. Louve would tell him—or not. Depending on the circumstances. Nicholas understood that more than most others.

He patted the horse's side. 'Farewell, my friend.'

Louve nodded, mounted his horse and joined the others.

The sun was cresting the horizon now. Into the thin grey haze came the din of opening shutters, and people filled the courtyard.

Impatient to be off, Reynold hurried his men through the gates.

Nicholas felt something of that same impatience now—but not to leave. To bound up the stairs towards the woman he loved.

And that was what he'd do.

Chapter Seventeen

'You didn't go.'

Nicholas stopped in the doorway. Whatever he had been expecting, Matilda standing almost frozen in the middle of the room wasn't it. Julianna was in her cradle, lying on her back. Her finger was in her mouth and her eyes were sleepy.

'What do you mean?'

'Reynold's troops are riding out through the gates.'

She wasn't surprised about Reynold. She was surprised about *him*.

'And you thought I'd go with them?'

She shrugged. 'You talked—'

'About what?' he asked.

She was failing at remaining calm. She blamed the way she'd used to be. Impulsive. Reckless.

'About the dangers of Reynold and your mercenary life. We both know you'd rather be going with them.'

'I have never said that.' He took a step closer. 'In fact everything I have said…and done…has indicated that I'm staying.'

'Staying and *wanting* to stay are two different things.'

He shook his head—once, twice. 'You think I'll leave again?'

'Can you blame me?'

'Without a doubt—especially considering our conversation after you tried to kill yourself on a horse.'

'I *didn't* try to kill myself on a horse.'

'We will continue to disagree on that, Matilda.'

'And what does that conversation have to do with you leaving?'

'Everything!'

He expected her to understand his emphatic response. She didn't. They'd argued after the horse incident. He'd said things that had made her realise her feelings for him weren't one-sided, and then Reynold had shown up.

Matters between them weren't settled. Not after a few words and some stolen moments in each other's arms. And yet he was acting as if they were.

Was this another reflection on her broken ability to trust?

She closed her eyes. She didn't want to see Nicholas's expression when she told him she was broken. Broken for ever, and with a complete inability to believe.

'This won't work between us. I'll keep doing this. Keep not trusting you.'

His expression didn't reveal wariness or pain. There was no anger or disappointment in his gaze. There was instead warmth. A kindness she hadn't thought him capable of.

'I know.'

'Then what?' she asked, not knowing the words she needed to say at this point. Her heart was breaking.

'I know you'll struggle with trust because I've

felt the same. I didn't have any trust, and then I trusted *you*.'

'And I failed you.'

'I trusted again, Matilda. When I held you, made love to you. When you became mine I trusted all over again.'

Half believing, and afraid to, she made a choked sound. 'Look what that got you—me thinking you'd leave.'

'And you still think I will?'

She blinked, searched her heart. 'Yes…'

'Yet still you stand here waiting for my explanation. Put your trust and your belief in that. There is a part of you that *wants* to learn to trust. Let it.'

Tears spilled and she wiped them away. 'I feel…broken.'

'Not broken. Changed. And it's those changes that make me want you more. Before, you trusted blindly. Now you know that trust comes at a price. You're wary of it. I was, too, but I realise that now my trust is stronger. Because despite everything it was found again.'

This conversation was so different from those

they'd shared in their youthful reckless love. Now they shared something else. It had once been broken, but it was mending. In that she believed.

She nodded.

A quick smile. Triumphant. Blinding. 'Good,' he said. 'But you don't know why?'

He had always been able to read her so well.

'This entire conversation makes no sense to me,' she said. 'Your returning from Reynold makes no sense. I'm questioning everything.'

'It's because you've changed, Matilda. And I've told you I want you *because* of those changes. Can you not accept the way *I* have changed?'

Changed? Physically he was as immense as ever. He still trained as he had in the past—even more now, and with skills she never would have imagined in all her days.

'I don't see it,' she answered truthfully.

'Despite the fact that it's carved across my face?'

'That's—physical. I've changed physically as well.'

His eyelids grew heavy. 'I know...'

She made an exasperated sound.

'I haven't received a scar since, Matilda. Why do you think that is?'

'Because you stopped fighting?'

He laughed. 'Hardly! Because I didn't make that same reckless manoeuvre again.'

'You did it to save Rhain.'

'I can see now that I was blinded by emotion at the time. Had I been more sensible, I could have killed that man without using my body as a shield.'

He was half-blinded because he loved his friend, had been trying to protect him, would have done anything to save him.

'So you've got better at the sword?'

He shook his head. 'I've got better *inside*. I've changed from how we were when we were young.'

'Are you're saying you're *sensible*?' She arched a brow.

'I'm not sensible at all. And there are many reasons why. I have made a deal with Reynold of Warstone. A man doesn't make deals or bargains with men such as he. Many are incapable of doing so. Even the King himself has to negotiate with that family, and often he's the more disadvantaged.'

'What did you do?'

'The same as I have done for the last six years—what I have done since my home started crumbling. I wrested back any bit of control I could and made the best of it. Sometimes I've been lucky, and I've earned enough coin so my home can stand and my tenants can have the tools they need. Sometimes I've lost an eye...'

He looked over her shoulder.

'This agreement with Reynold is somewhere in between. I played a part in the death of his brother. Reynold did not kill me for that, so I owe him a debt. He wants me to do something and I will—but in my own way. If we are lucky we will have more fortune coming our way for our children. If not, we will lose our lives.'

'That's too much risk when the factors are unknown.'

'Sometimes risk can be fun. Don't you remember?'

'I lost much when *I* risked.'

He gestured with his hands. 'Look at me, Matilda. I am larger than many men. I'm trained to be a warrior and my size and my strength are unparalleled. I am scarred from many battles. I am marred from throwing myself onto a sword meant for another. I am the least sensible man you will ever meet. So it should finally sink into that stubborn head of yours that I mean to stay here. In this home. *Our* home.'

Nicholas wasn't sensible. He was too full of risk and mischief. She'd witnessed it on seeing him with Reynold and seen it in his play with Agnes.

However, the old Nicholas wouldn't have had the patience to show a young girl how to build, nor chopped vegetables in her father's home. Even Bess had warmed to him—not because he helped more, but because he was different. Calmer. He would never be a farmer like Roger. He appreciated the land, but it wasn't part of him. And yet he was telling her he was staying?

Not possible. He was only here because Reynold had been here. Because risks had been brought to his front porch and he'd fought them.

'Tell me the truth,' she said. 'Does knowing that danger is now hovering over Mei Solis make it easier for you to stay.'

'Not in the way you think. I love it that I can stay, train more men, prepare for whatever battle Reynold brings to my home. I was made for this. And I love it that I have a use for my skills here. That makes it easier for me to stay because it gives me purpose, but it has no bearing on my decision to stay. Even if Reynold had never brought threat, I was made for this. I was made for *you*. Mei Solis was never my home but you were—you *are*. I've shown you how I've changed in the past. I'm not so feeble-minded as to think I won't change again, but I *intended* to change. To mould and pound the metal that was in me so that I fitted here long before he arrived. Long before he charged me with his secret.'

'I wouldn't want you to force yourself—'

'I do not force myself. I'm a broken sword without you. By staying here, by changing, I'm melting and pounding to change myself. To make me stronger and more worthy of you.'

'But you like to travel. To have and be surrounded by grand things.'

'In that we agree. And you're it. Please believe me now. You're *it*. You always have been, and I was a fool not to recognise it and hold it tight. I realise it now. Do you?'

At her silence he tugged his fingers through his hair.

'You don't. Let me explain… Even if Reynold gave me no choice but to pay my debt by leaving, I wouldn't go. I wouldn't leave. This time I wouldn't survive without you. I wouldn't want to.'

He *had* changed in the years since he went away—if he could accept and love the changes in her, why couldn't she accept the changes in him? Acknowledge them.

And he had said that Mei Solis wasn't his home. That his home was her. But she realised that it was more than that. The people here were his home as well. He'd changed not because the land had required him to, but because of the people. He was different with his tenants. There was a certain camaraderie between them now.

Nicholas took a step towards her. 'I will find help for your father. There are many healers in London. We'll find one who wants a country life. On the days when he is well, he won't even know the help is there, but on the days he is not he or she will be with him.'

'Rohesia has been asking for help...'

'All the better, then.' He took another step. 'And we'll find a way to help Agnes so she can build and draw to her heart's desire. I met many artists on my travels. Most of them were gaunt and looking for residence. We'll bring someone here for her.'

'She's just a girl.'

His lips curved. 'I won't tell the underfed artist if you don't—and if he gets restless because he teaches a girl, we'll let Julianna terrorise him for entertainment.'

Both were wonderful solutions. But... 'That won't help Mei Solis. It'll empty your coffers.'

'Our coffers will be full for ever. I wrote to Helena when you gave birth to Julianna and asked her to release the debt.'

'Why would you do such a thing? All those

years away, your father's death, all those years when Louve sent coin would be all for nothing.'

'Never for nothing, because I have learned a lesson from it. I have realised what my grandfather and my father did not. You were correct. Mei Solis isn't stones or dirt. It's the people. You and Julianna have taught me that. I understand now what you said to me before I left all those years ago. *"Who cares if the manor is crumbling as long as we have each other?"* I care—but have I learned the lesson too late?'

Another step, but he was still too far away. How could he be in any doubt?

'For *you*. Is all of this too late for you?'

'If I was still married to Roger it would be.'

'Not true. It would have been too late even if you hadn't married Roger, and I had not become a mercenary and lost my eye. We loved, but it has taken something stronger to make us the way we are now.'

'So many changes... I can hardly grasp it.'

He nodded solemnly. 'It's only sudden because we've been apart all these years. But each of those changes has brought us here. However, it means nothing if you don't agree. *Please* tell me you agree.'

Nicholas's gaze riveted her, as it used to, but there was so much more in it. The warmth was still there, but there was longing with that love. Vulnerability when there never had been before.

'Moreover,' he said, his voice low and filled with some promise, 'what use would it be if I made a deal with Reynold and no good came from it?'

He truly meant it, and there was a light of humour and mischief in his eye. It called to her.

Humour. Risks. And home.

Taking the remaining steps, she pressed herself into the warmth of his arms. This was something they hadn't had before. Something new, good and enduring. And she knew with all her heart exactly what it was.

'I love you.'

She felt Nicholas release his breath, and relished hearing his heartbeat increasing under her ear.

'I always did. But whatever this is inside me now...'

So much to say and she didn't know how to say any of it. At any moment Julianna would wake up, and words needed to be said, but they failed her completely. She felt *so* much.

'Matilda…?' He paused. 'I like the room.'

Her heart was already so full she wasn't prepared for his humour, and a laugh escaped her.

'I like it that you had the chairs and the bed made big enough for me, you and Julianna. And for Bess, Agnes, your father and Rohesia too.'

Humour…mischievousness.

All that was in her as well, and he should know it. Now that she'd found it again she didn't want to lose it. She wouldn't rein herself in for anyone any more.

'I was thinking Louve too,' she teased.

He growled. 'So those rumours are true? You had both Roger and Louve pursuing you?'

'Look at me—what do you think?'

He studied her face as if he was seeing it for the first time. 'They would have been fools otherwise. So I am glad Louve is gone.'

'Louve is *gone*?'

'With Reynold. It was time.'

'Long past.'

She held him closer, as if the very thought of someone leaving made her crave his staying. She revelled in the warmth, and he held her just as tightly.

'It's different, isn't it?' he said. '*We're* different this time.'

She nodded against his chest. 'And it's good.'

'Very good,' he said, with a promise in his voice that she recognised.

He was staying, and they would grow barley and turnips, and they would race horses. Julianna would follow Agnes, who'd teach her how to draw. Her father would have someone to care for him, and Rohesia would have her much-needed rest.

After all these years, all this change and adversity, she and Nicholas had found each other by laying aside their pride and daring to trust.

'*Very* good,' she repeated, tilting her head back for his kiss. 'But not always...'

* * * * *

LET'S TALK

Romance

For exclusive extracts, competitions
and special offers, find us online:

f facebook.com/millsandboon

⊙ @millsandboonuk

🐦 @millsandboon

Or get in touch on 0844 844 1351*

For all the latest titles coming soon,
visit millsandboon.co.uk/nextmonth

*Calls cost 7p per minute plus your phone company's price per
minute access charge

Want even more
ROMANCE?

Join our bookclub today!